THE DUBIOUS HEIR

"Is this still part of some game we are playing?"

She smiled a thought. "Yes, we are still playing the game. A bondage game and I will be your master. You must do as I say or I will be forced to whip you."

Dale smiled and licked his lips in anticipation.

Then she helped him put his pants and boots on. To him this was a sign that the game should be over. "What kind of game is this anyways?"

Treea stroked the side of his cheek softly and kissed his lips. "I'm taking you home."

"That is not part of the bargain. I do not go home with any of my clients."

"Well now, there is a first for everything. You're coming home with me and that's that. You are my prisoner and I am your captor. Now up on your feet and let's go."

Dale hesitated until he felt the blade at his back. He didn't remember seeing her carrying a knife of any kind. How did she do that?

Hi Readers!

Become a Beta Reader!

First come first serve. Not a contest! No purchase necessary.

Visit Lydia's website and fill out the contact form with your name and address.

As soon as the next book is ready to release you will receive the ARC copy for free. All Lydia asks is that you consider providing a review of the book on either GoodReads, Amazon, Barnes & Noble, or post the review on your blog.

Your feedback is valuable!

THE DUBIOUS HEIR

Lydia Clark

New Ipswich, NH

United States

http://www.lydia-clark.com/

Keelaa B Publishing

ACKNOWLEDGMENTS

Special thanks to my local RWA Chapter, you girls are the best. I also want to thank those who continued to encourage me to finish writing this story.

CHAPTER 1

Dale Montey flexed his biceps and admired himself in the mirror. The women loved him. It had to be his muscles he was sure of it. His flowing brown hair could have something to do with it too. As long as he kept his ears covered or they would know he was a half-breed, which was why he kept his hair long like a woman's. If he tied it back in a ponytail, his pointed ears would give him away.

It's not that the women don't like elves, he was just overly conscious about his pointy ears. His mom told him the elven part was from her side of the family. The genes were two generations removed, making him not officially a half-breed, but those who saw his ears thought differently none the less.

A quick spurt of Cardome on his chest would do it. It was one of those enticing scent lures he had picked up from the potion shop. It came in handy in his line of work. Not only did men like to play but women also liked to romp about and would pay a good price for an experienced man or Halfling as in his case. It paid his way through college.

The bottle of Cardome was almost empty he would have to buy more when he returned in the morning. Hopefully, this bit lasted him all night. It would make his job easier.

His client was to meet him at the Black Line Tavern at sundown. It had been prearranged by an undisclosed person. Just as well. The fewer people he knew on the finding end, the better. Last thing he wanted was to be thrown into the dungeon for prostitution.

He donned a grey broad-brimmed hat and a dark scarf for around his neck to keep the chill away. A button down leather shirt was slid on next to match his suede britches. The snake skin boots were next with their two-inch heel making him even taller than he appeared to be. Dale had been instructed that his client liked tall men.

A crooked walking stick completed his outfit. He gave the fireplace a quick poke with this same stick being satisfied they were nothing but coals and out the door he went into the cold night. His mom was asleep in her bed in the corner, never once stirring. It was best that she didn't know what his line of work was, saving her from the possible embarrassment.

Bats flew above the gas lamp lights being lit as he walked down the cobbled street. The workers paid him no heed while they buzzed about doing their nightly task.

Stone buildings lined the streets in such a pattern one could become lost in the maze of streets and cobble paths. The college campus was cramped for living space. Every room was taken while school was in session. The classes ranged from Alchemy to the white magic healers, being taught by witches and a warlock or two. A Sorcerer was the college president. That would be Professor Pyer, a very notable gentleman from the years of a great war.

The magic classes were taught in secrecy due to the

Duke's views about the matter. The white magic was referred to as herbalism and healers. The fact that the King's wife had died mysteriously of some unknown illness prompted the king to give special permission to the college to train such individuals in the healing arts. His belief had been that had a healer been present, they may have been able to save the life of his wife. Her death had happened two years prior.

Permission was granted against the Duke's liking and licenses to teach were given to only certain individuals by the King. This alone made the college the most sought out school in the land. It was why Dale needed to resort to such a profession to pay for his education.

The tavern now loomed ahead. Dale held the door for two goblin patrons exiting the establishment. He gave them a quick nod as they hurried on their way.

Thick smoke filled the room from cook fires and tobacco filled pipes. His eyes burned for a moment while they adjusted to the dim lighting. A cough had escaped his lungs before he was able to fight off the spasm from the smoke. He almost didn't see her sitting toward the back of the room. She was waiting just like was said.

She wore a leather skin dress. The bodice fit her figure like a glove making him ponder how he was going to get it off of her. It also evoked his manhood. It was rising to the occasion and ready for action. Her breasts bulged against the dress and pucker at the deep v-neckline exposing white skin and deep cleavage that could accommodate his manhood in a playful way.

Blonde curls splayed about her shoulders lightly. Her hair was long enough to use to tickle her fancy or the protruding nipples peeking from underneath her dress.

"What a beautiful night to find a fine lady as yourself in an establishment such as this." Dale extended his hand to lift hers to his lips for a tender kiss.

She smiled and let a little giggle slipped from her lips.

His cologne wafted toward her and immediately began to do its job making her feel a small twitch between her legs. It was potent. She had never experienced anything like it before.

Dale took the seat across from her. He did not know if they were to engage in small talk first or if they were going to get down to the bottom of their business. He could see she had already eaten by the looks of the plate on the table before her.

"Would you like me to call the barmaid? Have you eaten?"

"I will take a jug of mead with me when we leave. But my food this evening will be you." Dale licked his lips in anticipation of the night's activities.

"So you will." She agreed.

A minstrel began playing a quick step tune.

"Do you dance?" She asked.

"I can if that is what you wish."

He reached for her hand and led her onto the floor and began a fast waltz with one arm about her waist the other he held her hand. Their closeness only made his cologne stronger. She pressed her body against his.

The heat of her body excited him more and soon he began to forget where they were. His lips sought out her neck and he began to kiss her down her neckline making her dance steps falter.

"We need to go." He whispered in her ear. "Or at least find the shadows."

He led her off the floor and stopped by the bar for his jug of mead to take with him to the room upstairs.

<h1 style="text-align:center">CHAPTER 2</h1>

"All hands wanting to go a-shore, should do so while they can," Captain Pellesi called out to the crew on deck while they finished tying the boat to the moorings. "That goes for you too, Sweetie Pie."

"Pop, I think I want to stay behind," Treea replied to her father.

"Are you feeling all right child?" Captain Pellesi asked as he pressed the back of his hand to his daughter's forehead.

Treea pushed it away. "I'm fine Pop. I just don't feel like going into town. You go and have a good time." She looked across the deck and caught sight of the first mate Hurley while he gave a final tug on the rope he had been securing. He looked up in time to catch her looking at him, and scowled. "But bring me back some of that sweet bread."

"I will, love, and that of their cheeses too." The Captain turned and addressed the first mate. "Hurley will you join me into town?"

Hurley nodded. "Aye, sir. Indeed I will." He continued to scowl at Treea.

This did not go unnoticed by the Captain. "Don't tell me you two are at it again."

Treea opened her mouth to speak but held her tongue.

"Hurley, let's go."

"Aye. It will do some good to get away from the ship for a while."

Treea and Hurley were almost always fighting over some silly thing. Captain Pellesi would be the one to break the two apart in the middle of a heated argument. He wasn't sure as to which one would win if there were blood to be shed. He wanted to bet on his daughter. Her beauty would stall any man's hand for the seconds it would take for her swift sword to come down on her opponent's neck. The Captain taught her well.

It wasn't hard for the captain to notice how Hurley had a soft spot for Treea. Captain Pellesi had his suspicions about the two for the past few months. He hadn't caught them yet. Sometimes it was the way Treea looked at the first mate or how Hurley looked at her. The Captain knew that look. It was the same way he had looked at his own wife of many years before her passing some time ago.

He wasn't sure what he would do if he learned that the two of them were together as man and wife. Would he accept the arrangement? Or did he feel that Hurley was just too old for his daughter?

Though, they shouldn't be together anyways in that sense. His daughter was supposed to be off limits to all the men on his ship. Including the likes of Hurley. It was one of the reasons the captain wished he could find her a little apartment in the town and keep his trade route close to home.

Hurley was only ten years younger than the Captain.

He could almost pass as her Pop. Didn't she deserve to be with someone of her own age?

There were a couple of others on board who would be better suitable for her if only they were a lot smarter. Treea liked intellect. Hurley was smart, the Captain gave him that much credit. Should that be enough to go on for a man to be all that good for his daughter? Captain wanted more for her.

She deserved more.

A crowd of twenty men followed their captain off the ship leaving two men and the captain's daughter behind to keep watch. The men hated leaving Treea behind, but it didn't matter whether she was on board ship or out with them at a tavern, she never had any problem defending herself no matter what. Skilled in fencing at a young age of ten, she had joined the ranks of the crew three years ago when her mother passed away. She'd been just a young 'un at the time, sixteen birth years to be exact. Captain Pellesi didn't have to take her with him on board the ship. She was of age to put her up for a hefty dowry, but he believed in true love and wanted the same for his daughter, he just didn't want her to be alone.

Sailing was his third love, Treea's mom was his first and she was his second.

A sea captain by nature, it was what he loved to do. He, himself a mercenary, took odd jobs offered by various countries. The jobs were to either retrieve a relic or stop a shipment from being made or merchant trading as what the King had him do recently with the Norbese Clan. Some considered him a hero and others called him a Pirate. A notorious Pirate known around the world.

The tavern was not far from the ship. Looks from passerby's let the crew hands know how the townspeople regarded them. Some of the looks were contemptuous and others were excited to see them. Those excited to see them knew they brought welcome supplies of spices and teas. To seal the deal, they needed to see Ager Wells, the merchant who specialized in mercenary shipments at the Black Line Tavern.

If all else failed then he would have to resort back to the black market trades, as long as he didn't get caught.

Not all taverns were as large as this particular one and as well lit either. Each table held an oil lamp, tables long enough to seat ten men on each side. Two hundred men could fill the room, eating, drinking, or womanizing the waitresses. It did not matter whether they are human, goblin or elf. Some of the waitresses were nightly companions for a price. Prostitutes without the title. They were offered as escorts for companionship. These waitresses were available to the travelers at a hefty cost as part of the tavern's perks, making it the most popular venue in the city.

As soon as the Captain and his crew entered the inn another group rose from the table, paid and left, freeing up space. Nods and greetings were passed about on their way to the table as it was being cleared by their goblin waitress for the night. She was short and stout and full of vigor and hopes of making a substantial tip at the end of the night.

"What may I get you and your men tonight?"

"Bring us the house."

The waitress clapped her hands together, delighted to have the best patrons of the night. "Leg of lamb, goat cheese, boar's head, and plum pudding bread will be right out. Do you want your regular along with that? The jug of mead?"

"Aye, lassie, a large jug of mead will be good, and a romp with you later." The Captain reached out and smacked his hand gently against the goblins rump and gave it a provocative rub. She let out a quick giggle and hurried away into the kitchen to gather the fixings for her patrons.

"How can you carry on with a goblin?" Hurley asked as soon as the waitress was out of earshot.

"Easy," replied Tyler, a deck hand, "put a sack over her head and turn out the light."

The table sounded with hand slaps on wood and bold laughter.

"Aye, what makes you so sure it will be that goblin I will be taking up with later?"

"Well." Hurley mimicked the captain's hand movement on the goblin's arse in the empty air beside him. "What else am I to think?"

The crew laughed again.

"Go ahead and laugh. You see that one over there?" The captain pointed to a young maiden elf tending another table across the room. She did not look happy with her patrons, a group of king's men. "She will be my mark for tonight."

"That we'll have to see." A voice announced directly behind the captain.

Heads turned, the room went silent.

"Duke Ellington, what a lovely surprise. What brings you in this neck of the woods?" Hurley asked pleasantly.

"Why, it's your captain."

"Oh? What is it that you need of our Captain?" Hurley asked.

Duke Ellington opened up the scroll and read: "Captain Pellesi, you are hereby ordered under arrest by the King of Luxonbulm for piracy. Guards seize him."

CHAPTER 3

"Aye, lassie, I hate to tell you this but your father taint coming back." The first mate reported once he found her on board the Sea Wench.

"What do you mean, not coming back?" She crossed her arms across her chest. The fight she had with Hurley this morning before the sun up was now long forgotten. Her demands for him to come forward and tell her Pop about the two of them, no longer was important to her.

"It's exactly what I meant it to mean. He's been taken by the King's men."

Treea's heart sank to the pit of her stomach. There had to be some mistake. Why would the King's men take her father?

"But I don't understand. You were only going into port to sell our goods and bring back supplies. We are to set sail when the sun is up." Tears forced their way to the corners of her eyes. "How could you let this happen?" She bit her lip to prevent it from trembling.

"There wasn't a thing I could do. They swarmed

about him the minute he set foot into the tavern. As if they were lying in wait for him. Ambushed I say."

"But what did they want with him? Why did they take him? Did he steal something? What cause did they have to take him?" Treea fought the tears back with anger. She was sure it was all a misunderstanding and she would get to the bottom of it.

"Lassie, when will it sink in? Your Pop is a Pirate, always has been and always will be. They took him because of that formality."

"I will hear none of this. My father is a merchant and does legal business. He is not a Pirate." Treea put her hand upon her the hilt of her sword for gesture and began to depart the ship.

The first mate reached out and grabbed hold of her upper arm and held fast. "Lassie, you are not to go there. They will take you too."

"I've done nothing wrong."

"You are a woman and you are angry. You will cause more problems for your Pop than is needed. We will find a way. A different way to deal with this, I promise. I will go back into town and seek help. Someone must know what we can do. Secrets always lie in wait in the taverns after hours. I can do this better knowing you are still on this ship and safe. I will be back before dawn."

"And what am I to do if they take you too?"

"If I'm not back by dawn, hoist anchor and set sail out to a safe distance and keep watch. Something is not right and I hope to learn that we are not on the wrong side of things."

Treea watched the first mate walk down the plank and onto the dock. Before long he was far down the dark cobbled street and out of sight. She would wait and watch just like he said to do. He was right as always. Something was amiss. May Acionna watch over all of them and keep them safe.

The rest of the night followed with Treea giving orders for watch shifts to be set. They needed to keep vigil in case of a sudden attack. It seemed odd that the King's men would take her Pop and let the rest of the men go. If one were a pirate, the rest of them was also. These men were dedicated to her Pop, their captain of the ship. He had led them across the sea many times and not with the intent to catch fish either.

Most times a merchant ship would let them board and take their plunder uninhibited. Her Pop's reputation from his younger years was known from one captain to the next. The flag that was flown from the mast was his signature. No one ever was hurt and the merchant was allowed to keep half of his merchandise. It was always a fifty-fifty agreement they would eventually settle for with no battle or squander.

Her Pop said they weren't doing anything wrong but just charging for the use of the waters as a means of travel. These were their waters and they had the right to charge for safe passage. That was all they did.

So why did the King decide after all this time that her Pop had done something wrong? If the first mate did not come back with an answer, she indeed would find one on her own.

There was one thing she could do while she waited for Hurley's return. A protection spell would suffice and maybe keep their ship hidden from the eyes of danger. Just a little something to ease her fears. It didn't matter if the kingdom frowned upon women using magic of any kind. The Duke in particular would be after her head for using it. The King, not so much. He had mixed feelings about magic in general.

Apparently the spell worked. They had no unwanted visitors during the middle of the night and Hurley returned just before the sun up.

CHAPTER 4

Hurley was waiting impatiently for this moment. He'd been planning this for months. Finally, the captain was removed from duty. Now Hurley would soon control the ship and the crew. All he'd left to do was deal with Treea. But how was he going to do that? Have her arrested just like her Pop, kill her, no he couldn't do that, or find a way to control her emotionally. The later might be the easiest. Especially with the relationship he had already established with her over the past few years. For Pete's Sake, she was a woman, and he was a man, how hard could it be to gain full emotional control? To be able to make her do anything, absolutely anything he wanted her to do, like letting him take over the command of the ship?

She'd been on the ship working alongside the rest of the men for the past three years. Her status had grown to his equal. He hated to think that she may have surpassed his equal, though lately, the captain had been confiding in Treea more than him, which Hurley thought was not right. He was the first mate, not Treea, and he was a man and she a woman. A ship was no place for a woman.

When she'd boarded the ship that first time, her beauty struck all the men and Captain Pellesi made certain that she was known to be off limits to all the men on the ship. The captain wanted her married to a good man. The life of a seafarer was not what he wanted for his daughter. She deserved more and a much better man for a husband.

But the Captain's order fell short on Treea. She pursued Hurley by spending time with him in close quarters. It all started with a subtle look, a twist of a lock of hair around her finger and a soft touch of her hand on the side of his stubbled face. An untimely wave crashing into the side of the ship sent her body against his own ending in an embrace and that first kiss below deck in the hold. The feel of her body against his own triggered a lust that had never been fulfilled until she came along.

He thought of Treea while the guards led her Pop, the Captain away. Hurley tried to plan out what he was going to say to her when he got back to the ship. How was he going to break the news to her? Surely she should understand that her Pop is a pirate and a well-known one at that. This day was inevitably coming. It was a wonder it hadn't happened years ago. How the man had managed to stay out of the sights of the King was beyond his knowledge.

Up until six months ago, when they had last docked at this port, the thought of Captain Pellesi being arrested never once entered Hurley's thoughts. Not once had he dreamed of this day or considered wanting to take over the reins of the ship. That was until the Duke approached him.

Duke Ellington approached Hurley on the day they were setting sail once again with a proposal. He wanted to hire Hurley to do some sort of job for him. Hurley turned him down at first. Saying how he was just a deck hand and nothing more, but the Duke pressured him, telling him he could give him anything he wanted if he would do this one favor for him.

Hurley tried to come up with an impossible answer by stating he wanted to be Captain of the Sea Wench. Not once did he ask what his task was to be in exchange for this prize. He figured by asking for such a thing the Duke would just give up and walk away. Which he did. Nothing else had been said. It didn't need to be. The Duke had just proven moments ago how he could deliver his promise.

Now that Captain Pellesi was arrested that made Hurley first in command.

What would he tell Treea?

Her Pop was in a tavern brawl?

No, she would see right through that answer.

Captain Pellesi had refused to pay for his woman and meal.

No, Treea would not believe that answer either.

The Captain was arrested for being a Pirate?

Maybe. It was the truth, even if she didn't want to accept it.

Hurley didn't waste any time. As soon as the Duke left the tavern with his men and the captain, he told the other's he needed to go and let Treea know about her Pop's predicament.

Hurley returned to the inn later. After he promised Treea, he would find someone who could help them with this matter. Outside the Tavern, a figure called to Hurley, calling him into the dark shadow of the building hidden from the light of the moon. It was that of a woman. "You want to help your Captain? This here book may help you with his release."

Hurley accepted the package, and before he could

give it back, the woman disappeared, leaving him holding it, bewildered. Who was she? Why would she want to help the Captain? What did the Duke want Hurley to do now that he had delivered his promise?

His only clue as the woman left was her shadow, definitely that of a goblin.

He never once expected any of this. The Duke promising him anything, nor the Captain's arrest. When he promised Treea he would find help to see to it that the Captain was released from prison, he never once expected someone would step forth from the shadows. Not with such an answer as this, being held within the book.

CHAPTER 5

"Well, what did you learn?" Treea asked over a plate of eggs.

Hurley tossed a small book on the table. It was leather bound and wrapped in paper tied with a thin cord. Treea pushed her plate aside and untied it, unwrapping the book. It was hand written. Even though Treea was the daughter of a pirate he had made certain that she had learned to be well read. She had no problem reading the handwriting in the book.

"I was given this."

"Did you look at it?" She asked Hurley.

"Why would I, you know I can't read." His brows scowled with his answer.

She always found his scowls, grins, smirks, and grimaces attractive. It was a good thing her Pop never found out or caught the two of them down below deck. If he did, Hurley would undoubtedly be reduced to a dead man with no chest to sit upon.

"It's a diary. What would I want with another

woman's diary?" Treea pushed the book away and went back to her breakfast. She hated to waste food. "Where did you get it?"

Hurley leaned back in his chair and watched her eat. "I can't divulge my source to you at this time. I was told to keep this book a secret. It holds the answer to getting our captain, your Pop free. Some sort of secret is in there that even the King knows nothing about."

"Really?" Secrets, Treea loved secrets especially when they belonged to others. She carefully carved an apple she had beside her plate. Her favorite fruit was saved for last. After cutting it into slices, she returned her attention to the book. Knowing there was a secret hidden within enticed her to begin reading.

Hurley watched her read and take dainty bites of her apple slices. He knew those lips and how they felt on his flesh. He had to leave or risk distracting her from this important task. There would be time later to frolic below the deck. "If you learn of anything, I'll be in my cabin napping."

Typically she would make a remark of sorts. For once she was too intent on finding this so-called mystery and secret that would save her Pop. This was more important than rolling around on the floor for a little bit of frolicking fun.

She read the diary page by page. It was written by a very young woman who was yet to grow into her prime. She was barely childbearing age. A chambermaid who found the favor of the young prince who was soon to be crowned king. Each page read of her heart stirrings for the Prince and his for her. How they would meet in the middle of the night when all the castle was still and sleeping. They would steal off into places where no one would come across them or hear them. Many times it was in the stables where they would meet. The horses would snicker softly while the couple's sounds of pleasure would escape from their lips in the silent night.

Treea came across a passage that told of one of these so-called nights when they met in the stable. After reading a few more words, Treea knew she would have to read this diary in a more private setting. The most private being her own cabin. She slipped the book underneath her shirt, tucking it into her waistband to prevent anyone from noticing it. There were a secret and a mystery within this book, but the strong desire of the young woman writing, brought out a twitch between Treea's legs. An arousal all to its own.

Within the confines of her cabin, Treea was able to continue reading. The moon had been bright that night when the couple once again had met in the stable. The prince was as excited to see her as she was to see him. They came together in the tack room and wrapped each other into their arms holding fast while their lips met. Lust need and want all at the same time fueled their fire.

The young maid immediately felt the long hard manhood against her body when she was held fast. As they continued kissing he slowly walked her backwards until her back was up against the wall where he began pressuring his groin harder and harder against her. The barriers of their clothing were preventing its entrance into her womanhood.

He moved his lips to her neckline and began to remove parts of clothing from her body first exposing her milk-white breasts and their hard young nipples. He could not ignore these. His lips moved from her neck down between her breasts and then to each nipple. Sucking gently at first, then harder and harder. Teasing each one with his teeth.

By now the young maid had removed his shirt, and his pants were unlaced, hanging below his knees. She did not have to search for his manhood. It stood at attention waving before her. When she set her fingers to it, she found it pulsed in her hand. It was hot and smooth and the veins bulged close to the hard head.

She wasn't quite sure what she was supposed to do at this point. They had never gone this far before. It felt right. So she followed her instincts and knelt before her prince and set her tongue against the hard head and licked it gently. She looked up once to see if he approved. His head was back and his mouth was open while his hands continued to rub her nipples. Tenderly pinching each one pulling them in a teasing fashion.

A wetness formed between her legs that made her unsure of herself.

Treea stopped reading long enough to remove her own top and pants and laid in her hammock with her blanket close by. With her index finger, she slowly stroked her mound between her legs. Her own wetness matched the young maiden. She had to go back to reading and stroking at the same time.

The young maid took the Princes manhood into her mouth making him harder still. His hands left her breasts and found the top of her shoulders and began to pull her on and off his cock. Now she knew why the older girls referred to this part with such a word. Rock and cock were not that far off and his was a rock hard cock. She continued to let him move her mouth up and down, her tongue stroking him each time. A small trickle ran down her throat she was not expecting and almost began to choke.

That was how he knew she had enough of that. He quickly pulled her to her feet and turned her around to face the wall, placing her hands on it with his own. Rubbing his cock against the inner of her thighs and against her womanhood. She was not expecting to feel the sensation she felt when he did this. It made her twitch and ache for what she had no idea of. Not until he took one hand and angled his cock against her and began to slowly push himself inside.

It hurt at first, but her body wanted it too. Once he passed her barrier and was in she let out a gasp. Once again, his fingers found her nipples and began to roll them gently sending ripples through her body while his lips set against the flesh of her neck behind her earlobe that his tongue began to tickle.

The Prince continued to grind into her in such a way that her body shook from the pleasure, Treea began to insert her own finger into her hole and slowly worked it in and out while she read. Her juices flowed and her canal pulsed against her finger. The feeling excited her so much she had to set the book down and insert two fingers. She slowly worked them in and out of her body while she groped at her own breast with her other hand. She envisioned the prince to be like that of Hurley. She would never forget how his cock felt inside her while they were below deck while the ship was out at sea. He pushed harder and harder into her with each rolling wave while she straddled on top of him riding him as if he were a horse. She'd pull off his cock just far enough to keep him from falling out before gorging him deep inside her once again until the internal waves would overcome both of them. Her canal would pulse while his cock pulsed and his juices shot deep inside her.

It always was over too soon. This seemed to be the young maids complaint too. She wanted more of him only to find it would not happen. The manhood had retired for the night. The prince promised to meet her there every night and exchange their juices again and again.

But it didn't happen. In fact three nights later the Prince was moved from that part of the castle to another wing and was forbidden to have any access to the young maid. He had been hidden from sight.

Then the announcement came. The Prince was to marry Princess Lorila from the Kingdom of Perth. After the wedding, the Prince was to be crowned King so his father would be allowed to step down and enjoy a brief retirement before his life was cut short mysteriously. Poison so it seemed. No one could prove it. So it remained a mystery.

During the following months, the young maid began to feel bloated in her lower abdomen. At first she thought it was the lack of exercise with her young prince. But her stomach began to grow month by month. She kept her figure hidden fearing some illness had taken over her. Then the movement in her stomach happened. It was a ripple. She lifted her top when she was alone in her room and watched her round belly move. Her belly was hard as her Princes cock had been that night so long ago. How many months had gone by since they had last met? She could barely see her feet, her belly stuck out so far. It was surprising no one else had noticed her figure while she continued to work at the castle. Or so she thought.

Two weeks later the Duke of Luxonbulm approached her and asked her a question. It shocked her. "When is the baby due?"

"I dear say, I don't know what you are talking about." She said to him.

"I think you do. Should the King and Queen find out about you, something bad will happen to both you and your illegitimate child. Take care."

He walked away leaving her to ponder his words while shock took over her mind.

She was with his child and never once considered that this could happen. The Duke was right. She had to leave the castle before anyone else found out.

In the middle of the night, she packed her bag of few belongings and slipped out of the gates undetected. She had traveled for hours in the night before she came across a town. The tavern had a stable and she took shelter there while the babe she carried in her belly came forth from her loins.

She named him in secrecy, Dale Montey. No one was to ever know that he was the illegitimate heir to the throne. If they were ever to find out both of their lives would be at stake.

Treea closed the book. "How touching. I wonder where this babe is now?"

CHAPTER 6

Hurley, the first mate, found Treea above deck leaning against the ship's railing looking out at the sleepy town before her. "What did you learn, lassie? Was there anything that could help in that their book?"

"Aye, there is an illegitimate heir somewhere here in this town. We need to find him."

"What do we do with this heir once we find him? If it's an illegitimate heir, there isn't much they can do for us."

"I was thinking," Treea's wheels were turning in her head ever since reading the last line in the book about the child's name. "Did the King and Queen ever have a child?"

Hurley thought long and hard. "No, I don't believe so. How would that help us?"

"If there was no child then that means there is no heir to the throne."

"So, you're thinking of exposing this illegitimate heir?"

"Not just that. We can capture them and hold 'em as hostage. We can ask for not only the release of my Pop but also for a ransom. Make them pay for what they have done to my Pop. He is a good man and shouldn't have been treated as a criminal."

"Aye, I couldn't agree more with you. How do you expect us to find this here heir?"

"Well, we do have a name. It is Dale Montey."

Hurley's eyes went wide. "Him?"

"Oh, so you know of this person?"

"I do. He is no better than a pirate." Hurley said with a broad grin on his face. "Come to think of it, I think I know just how we can get close enough to him to capture him." He touched a loose strand of hair hanging just below Treea's ear and used it to tickle her earlobe.

"How?"

"You are going to hire him for the night. I hear he is almost as good as me."

Treea squinted suspiciously at Hurley. She was not quite sure what he was hinting at.

"Believe me, you're going to really enjoy yourself. Just don't enjoy yourself too much." Hurley stroked a finger across the bottom of her chin tenderly. "Remember who you belong to."

"Are you insinuating that I belong to you?" Treea scoffed. "You should know me better than that by now. I belong to no man and will keep it that way, especially since you didn't want to tell Pop about us."

Hurley's smug grin dropped a notch. "I will arrange a meeting for you. I think three gold pieces will do. He may want more, but I think you will be more than he is bargaining for."

Treea watched Hurley depart the ship. She did not like the way he was trying to lay claim to her when he wouldn't confront her Pop about their relationship. Did he consider her to be his woman? If her Pop ever found out about the two of them on his own... Nope, she would never be his woman, since he didn't have the courage to come forward and say something to her Pop about the two of them, but she didn't mind being his playmate.

Who was this so-called heir and how was it that Hurley knew them? What was equivalent to being as a Pirate? Treea could only wonder. She continued to ponder for hours while she waited for Hurley to return with news of the heir and how they could be found.

By noon, the clouds grew grey and covered the sun. The temperature dropped. A severe storm was brewing, meaning they would have to move out to sea away from the docks in case of harsh waves and winds. Plus she did not need anyone to see her while she cast her spell of protection over the ship. It was one of the reasons her Pop had allowed her to join him aboard the ship.

Being a Sea Witch was not something one wanted just anyone to know about. Her Pop might be a prisoner in a dungeon, but if they knew she was any kind of witch then she would be burned at the stake. That would be such a barbaric way to die. She would rather die while in the throes of ecstasy.

"I found him at the Black Line Tavern. You are to meet him there in two hours. He will be expecting you. Sit in the far corner of the room and order a meal. I told him what you looked like and he will find you. Your time with him has already been paid for. I hope you do not overly enjoy yourself," Hurley chuckled when her expression turned sour once again when he mentioned about over enjoying herself.

"What did you pay for, might I ask?"

Hurley tipped his head playfully. "I think I will leave that as a surprise for you. Though, I'm sure you will figure it out once you see him." He whispered in her ear and kissed her on the back of her neck.

Treea glanced about the deck, she was fearful that someone would see them. Not a soul was in sight. Thankfully.

He continued. "When you have figured a way to capture this heir, I will be waiting out back of the Tavern to help bring him aboard the ship." He teased her once again. "Remember don't enjoy yourself too much." He traced a finger down her throat gently toward her bosom and stopped. This sent ripples of forthcoming excitement within her. Making her want to take him by the hand to lead him below. Now was not the time for this. She needed to find the Tavern on her own. "Oh and leave the sword behind, and wear a dress this once. You don't want to alert the soldiers of who you are."

Hurley was right about the sword. She took it off and left it in her cabin before departing in search of this Tavern where she was to find this heir. There was no need for her to call undue attention to herself.

She walked the streets following a map that Hurley was kind enough to provide for her. The city was set up like a maze of streets. Some going this way and others making one back track. Soon she knew why Hurley felt she needed a head start in order to find this Tavern. It was nestled in a remote area with access to it being by a street off by itself, but being in the middle of the city. It reminded her of setting a snare to capture an enemy. Who was the enemy in this case, her or the heir? Hopefully, he was to be a prisoner and not her.

The inn was busy, smoke and laughter filled. In the back corner as Hurley said was a vacant table. That was where Treea was to wait for him. She ordered a plate of food while she waited, just as she was instructed to do, and went about not calling attention to herself. This last part was sort of complicated. Being a woman and there in the tavern alone, many a man gave her an eye that she managed to deflect casually.

Had they know she used witch's magic on them to keep them at bay, they would have called the guard and she would have been taken immediately to be strapped to the stake. Witches were not tolerated in this land, making it best not to be caught in the act. The Duke would see to it. But had she been registered with the college, the King would have given her leniency.

It was a sad thing though, for the many women who had been wrongfully accused of such a crime and wrongfully burned for being in the wrong place at the wrong time. Those were the ones no one ever avenged. Those were the ones who continued to be scrutinized many years after their death. No one ever knowing the truth. Except for the guilty witch, who used the innocent to protect themselves from the horrific fate.

Time passed. Treea was close to finishing up her meal. That was when she spied him entering the establishment. For an illegitimate heir, he carried himself well and joked with many of the patrons on his way to her table. He was not what she was expecting to see. She expected a haggard young man living in rags or maybe that of a thief. Instead, before her stood a man with substantial stature who carried himself well. He even looked stately. Funny how Hurley never responded when she asked him what the surprise was supposed to be, except that she would know as soon as she saw him.

Hurley was right.

The way he looked at her made her feel uncomfortable. A ripple of excitement crept up from her stomach making her feel queasy and nervous, anxious for the night's event to come to an end. The dress she wore may have had something to do with this uneasy feeling. Dresses were not her usual attire. She wore this one at Hurley's request. So that the client would be able to find her in a crowded room.

She was surprised when she asked if he wanted to order a meal only to have him decline. But when he responded by saying she was going to be his meal, she had a vague idea to what he meant by that. He was the kind of man to say such a thing to her, being a gigolo.

Hurley set this meeting up without telling her that she was meeting a male harlot. It was what he was hinting at when he told her not to have too much fun.

Then fun was what she planned to do since Hurley told her not to do it. Which is why she asked him to dance with her. How else was she to put her mark off guard? She had to appear as though she were truly there to hire him for his services.

He danced with her in a way that sent her senses crazy, firing up lust deep down inside her. Witchcraft, it had to be that, it was the only answer. His aroma increased his attraction. She would have to counter this with her own little spell. Just by dancing closer to him set that spell in motion.

His lips touched her neckline and she could not help but begin to respond. It triggered responses in her that she could not shut off. Not like she normally could do. He must have some pretty powerful magic of his own.

Before she realized where they were going, he was leading her up a stairway above the tavern. Away from prying eyes, behind a closed door, his lips found hers while he pushed her up against the wall. His lust activated her lust. There was no stopping now.

What was her plan supposed to be? How was she going to capture him when all she could do was want him, excitement aroused between her legs.

She was the one who apparently was snagged in the net instead. She had to stop him before it was too late. But the way his lips felt on her skin made her nerves tingle. Her lust had turned to want. A want she could not shut off.

His hands found hers, he moved them up above her head, holding her prisoner against the wall. His tongue darted about her mouth tickling her own tongue with light strokes.

Treea broke off the kiss for a gasp of breath. His lips immediately moved to the middle of her neckline, gently caressing their way down to where her two white breasts held tight against each other by the cord of the dress of her bosom.

He used his teeth to untie it making her want him even more. Treea began breathing in small pants. She knew she had to stop soon or it would be too late. But the feel of his hardness against her made it impossible to stop. He used it well with skill to entice and tease her aiming it for the area between her legs where the feeling of it made her automatically spread her legs for him to find a home for his pride. A big long hard pride of manhood that would drive any woman crazy.

She had no intention of letting him continue. She thought of the chambermaid and the prince in the diary. Just as the young woman wanted she too wanted to see and touch it. By now her dress was down past her shoulders exposing her breast. His lips found her nipples and teased them with his tongue. Trailing in soft gentle circles around the base only to lick them up the middle to the tip making her let out a gasp she could not stifle.

Finally, he spoke again to her softly in her ear. "You want me as much as I want you."

Treea couldn't help but nod slowly. She did want him there was no doubt about that. He continued to hold her hands above her head. She was his prisoner. He was in control. With one hand holding both her wrists above her head, the other trailed down to undo his pants and let them drop to his knees exposing his long hard prime member. She didn't need to see it, she could feel it against her body.

His experience showed by the way he was able to hoist up her dress so quickly and tuck it out of his way finding an easy path to her womanhood. Kissing her as he inserted himself, slowly, gently, thrusting in and out. She wanted every inch of him.

One of her legs lifted up to his hip while he wrapped his free arm under her bottom supporting her weight.

The whole time he continued to hold her arms above her head while she moved her body in rhythm with his, seeking to send him deeper and deeper inside until he found her spot. The place that brought her over the threshold, the intensity never met by Hurley.

But she had not satisfied him. His endurance was high along with his erection. He released her arms and stroked her hair, brushing it away from eyes bright with pleasure. Treea was not done with him just yet either. Now it would be her turn. She knew a trick or two too.

"Sit," Treea said pointing to a chair set out in the middle of the room. He had watched her stroll about in her buff, no modesty at all. She knew her body had the curves men liked and knew how to move that body about him.

He sat as he was told.

"Your headband, pull it down over your eyes, no looking."

He smiled at the thought, carefully making sure not to expose his half-breed's ears. He loved these types of games. Not many women would play them with him.

Treea used her hair to tickle around his neck while she ran her hands from behind him down his chest, slowly moving about him letting a thigh touch teasingly at his thigh but always remaining in control.

While she continued to tease him, she looked about the room and spied a thin cord like the one in her dress. She retrieved it from a nearby table and took one of his hands and cinched it about his wrist. At the same time, she sat on his lap facing him, straddling his manhood under her. It throbbed hard in response to her touch of her body.

She proceeded to tie his wrists together behind his back, making sure as not to cut the circulation off but snug enough so he couldn't get away. Was she even sure that this was the guy she was supposed to capture?

There was only one way...

She spoke his name.

"Dale, are you enjoying yourself?" She tried to sound like one of the tavern wenches she had seen about the crew when they had visited the last port. All the men had disappeared upstairs with one except for her Pop. He said he had to keep an eye on her. She tried to reassure him that she could take care of herself, but he would not hear otherwise. Hurley waited as long as he could until he finally gave up and left with one of the wenches.

"Umm... that is what I am supposed to ask you, my queen bee."

She leaned close to his face and whispered in his ear. "So you are Dale Montey?"

"Yes, the very one. Who else could serve your needs better? Certainly not Hector the Red. I am the best gigolo in this here town."

Her questions were not affecting him in the right way. It was evident by the way he went limp. Treea had enough fun for now anyways. She left him sitting naked there in the chair while she dressed. Eyeing his body while she did so. His physic was very pleasing to a woman's eye. Biceps that rippled when they flexed. He was just well built all over.

"Are we done here so soon?"

Treea did not answer. She continued to re-lace her cord across the top of her dress pulling her breasts taut underneath it.

Dale stood and almost lost his balance knocking the chair off to the side by his stumble. "Do you mind removing my blindfold and undoing my wrists? I'd like to put my pants back on if you don't mind."

Treea uprighted the chair putting it back in place and directed him to sit. "Sit and I will help you dress."

"Is this still part of some game we are playing?"

She smiled a thought. "Yes, we are still playing the game. A bondage game and I will be your master. You must do as I say or I will be forced to whip you."

Dale smiled and licked his lips in anticipation.

Then she helped him put his pants and boots on. To him this was a sign that the game should be over. "What kind of game is this anyways?"

Treea stroked the side of his cheek softly and kissed his lips. "I'm taking you home."

"That is not part of the bargain. I do not go home with any of my clients."

"Well now, there is a first for everything. You're coming home with me and that's that. You are my prisoner and I am your captor. Now up on your feet and let's go."

Dale hesitated until he felt the blade at his back. He didn't remember seeing her carrying a knife of any kind. How did she do that?

When Hurley told her she couldn't take her sword, he never said she couldn't take the blade. She had strapped it under her dress on her ankle well out of sight. She had poked him one more time before he moved forward and out the door.

Hurley was waiting out behind the tavern just as he said he would. "What took you so long?"

Treea smiled. "A girl's got to do what a girl's got to do, especially since you didn't say what I had to do."

Hurley eyed her. He could barely make out her features in the dark. Her response was not to his liking.

He would have to deal with her when they got back to the ship. She might be the captain's daughter, but her tone did not sit well with him. She wouldn't be in charge much longer anyways. Not with what he had in mind.

The two of them led Dale back to the ship and shoved him down below in a holding hole. A ball and shackle were used to keep him from escaping. Bread and water would be provided come morning.

In the captain's quarters, the two began to argue over what they were going to do with their new found prisoner.

"I say we ask for my father and nothing more."

"What is wrong with you woman. We stand to get a lot of money for this man. We could buy your Pop's freedom ten times over. You even said so yourself."

Treea crossed her arms and turned her back on Hurley. She knew he was right, but it wasn't her idea so she didn't like it.

"Think about it Treea. You know I'm right. We're right. He is our only chance."

The room went silent. Only the sound of the waves hitting the side of the boat was heard in the room. Treea turned around to find that Hurley was gone. He knew how to win an argument.

CHAPTER 7

Hurley leaned against the side of the boat looking out over the pier. It was only a matter of time before his plan worked out. Everything was going as it should. The captain had been arrested and thrown in the dungeon. All he had left to do was get rid of the girl. Then the boat would be his.

So why bother trying to free the Captain if it meant giving back the command of the ship?

He had mixed feelings about the girl. Over the past few months, she started growing under his skin. She was more than just a mere plaything, which was all she was at first. That is, as long as her Pop didn't find out about the two of them.

It wasn't because her Pop didn't like Hurley. In fact, Captain Pellesi was like a second father to him. Taking him under his wing over twenty years ago, back when he was only twenty-four years old. That was the age Treea was now. Age would most likely be a major factor in how her Pop would feel about them if he knew their relationship.

So far, Hurley had managed to take care and not be caught. But now that her Pop, Captain Pellesi was out of the picture while he was sitting in the dungeon, it gave him not only free range of the ship but also that of Treea. The plan about Treea was the only part of the plan that was not coming together properly.

He had to find a way to make certain that Captain Pellesi was never going to be released without Treea becoming suspicious. Win her over and then the Captain position would be his. Just as he planned.

Sugar coating for Treea might go far.

"Hurley, I've come to say I'm sorry. You are right. We need to ask for the ransom and the release of my Pop."

Her voice caught him completely off guard. It was so unlike her to agree with him so readily. Hurley whipped around to make sure it was Treea's voice he had heard.

"What made you change your mind?"

"I don't know, it just sounds like the thing to do." Treea held out a large piece of rough paper with writing on it. "I wrote the ransom note. You just need to find someone to deliver it."

Hurley put his fingers to his mouth and let out a loud shrill whistle. A young boy came running. He couldn't have been more than fourteen years of age. "Marvin, you are to run this letter to the King. Make sure he gets it and return as quick as you can."

"Aye, Sir."

Marvin took the letter never looking to see what it said. He tucked it safely in his belt at his waist and ran off at a sprint for the castle. Quickly disappearing out of sight.

"Now we wait." Hurley turned back to look past the railing while the sleepy town woke while the sun began to rise behind them. A new day and the plan of his action was going as it should.

Treea slipped away without Hurley noticing she was gone. It didn't matter. He would be captain of the ship soon. His ship, his crew and Treea would be his wretched woman. Let her have her so called freedom while she could. It did not matter. She wouldn't go far.

CHAPTER 8

Treea did not like the way Hurley was acting, he seemed off and too quiet. Something was not quite right. Did he feel jealous for her being with the gigolo? He was the one who had set it up, so why was he acting this way. It didn't matter. He would be himself once again, soon, she was sure of it. Hurley was Hurley, he was also a man.

There was a captive down in the hold that needed tending to also. Since no one else was going to do it, this left Treea to the task of bringing food and water below to the prisoner.

"Hello – are you awake?" Treea called before setting foot on the floor. She held onto the ladder with one hand while balancing a platter of bread and cheese. A flask of water was tied to her waist.

The prisoner sat on a pile of burlap that was used for a makeshift bed. "Aye – I'm awake." He tugged at the chain attached to his leg. "Why am I being held? If you think, you can make me perform more services for you for free by holding me here captive then you have another thing coming. I won't do it."

Treea laughed. "You think I'm holding you for my own enjoyment? If it was only as easy as that." She pushed a piece of hair that had fallen out of her ponytail out of the way of her eyes and smiled a tender smile at her prisoner. She liked his way of thinking. A sex slave had never crossed her mind.

Morning light filtering down inside the hole allowing Treea to see her prisoner much better. He was bare-chested and muscular. Just the sight of his naked body sent a quiver of want across her body making it hard to forget how he had made her feel not too long ago.

"I brought you food and water." Treea stood just out of the prisoner's reach. She was afraid that if she were to allow him to touch her she wouldn't want him to stop, even if it were a life or death matter. So she set the tray of food along with a flask on the floor and gently pushed with her foot so that it was within his reach.

"If you're not keeping me as a sex slave then why am I a prisoner? It can't be for money, I have none. I'm just a poor bloke who is trying to pay his own way through college. Do you know how hard that is when you have to take care of your haggard mother?"

"Your name is Dale Montey, correct?"

"Aye, that's my name."

"You are the heir to the throne. We have kidnapped you. In exchange for your release, the king, your father, is to release my father from his dungeon."

Dale burst out laughing. He clutched at his sides from laughing so hard. "My father the king – I have never heard such a thing. "My mother told me how my father was a tailor who died before I was born. I had no father and had I had one he would never have been king. You have the wrong man."

"No, I don't have the wrong man."

"What makes you so sure?"

"The birthmark on your inside right thigh, I saw it last night as soon as you dropped your pants."

Dale's eyes narrowed. "What proof do you have, that I would be the heir?"

"I have your mother's diary from when she was a young woman. She described the birthmark you were born with."

"How would my mother have known the King? Why has she been living as a poor seamstress since I was born?"

"Because she had to flee the castle before you were born. She was afraid for yours and her life should the new queen discover the truth."

"Such an unbelievable tale. They will never believe you."

"Aye, but I have a book of truth and once the king sees it he will believe."

Treea hated it when other didn't believe a word she was saying. She snatched up the plate and left the food on the floor along with the water skin. "Eat up. Wasted food can be the death of you." With one hand holding the plate, she climbed the ladder leaving Dale alone in the hole to ponder over his new found lineage.

CHAPTER 9

"Your majesty, we have received a message for you. It is from the daughter of Captain Pellesi who is being held in the prison." The messenger paused waiting for the king to respond.

"Well read it!" The duke order when the King said nothing in response.

"Your majesty, you have taken my father into custody for no reason. He has done nothing to give cause for this action. I have requested once already that you release him, but since you have given me no choice, I have taken the liberty to hold your son. The only known heir to the throne, prisoner until you comply and release my father along with a sum of one hundred gold bars to pay for his wrongful arrest."

"What is this? I have no son. Give that to me!" The king stood and took the scroll from the messenger, sending him off on his way with a quick wave of his hand.

"How can she claim to have my son when the queen

never gave birth to one single child before she died."

"I'm sure it must be a hoax, Your Majesty," replied the Duke.

The king tried to think back in time. It had been so long ago. Back before he had married. There had been a young woman. How he had loved her and suddenly she had disappeared as though she had never existed. He had come close to telling his parents a declaration of love for this woman when he was told he were to marry a woman he did not know. But he had feared his father's reaction after he told him it was already arranged to keep the bordering country allied.

He had never known her name, this young woman, she had never said it and he had never asked. Had this been wrong of him? Even though he had not known her name, he still remembered her smell and smile and the way she made him feel when they were together.

She had disappeared just before the woman he was to marry arrived at the castle. It had been so mysterious, her leaving in the middle of the night.

"I'm sure you are right. But I do want you to look into this matter anyways. If there were an heir to the crown, then my people would be happier to know that they would have sound leadership to continue overseeing their kingdom."

"As you wish, your majesty." The Duke bowed and left the king's side allowing him to continue to think back in time, wondering what ever happened to the young woman he had loved so many years ago.

This would put a crux into a plan he already had in place for the kingdom. Should he still go through with it, or cancel the deal he had already arranged. He was surprised that Ellington was happy to go along with his arrangement as of so far since he had wanted the throne for many years.

CHAPTER 10

This was bad news. If an heir to the throne were found, it would mean that the Duke of Luxonbulm would never be crowned king. The Duke couldn't let this happen, after all, he was the Kings brother and should have been named king a long time ago. But his wretched brother stole the crown right out from under his nose by being their father's favorite. The man had always favored the younger of them.

For years following, he had made one plan after another to take over the throne. He had even taken such pain to make sure that the queen had never become pregnant by buying potions from an apothecary to prevent such a thing. Painstakingly he had made sure to mix this into her daily drink by telling the servant it was a medication to keep the queen thin and beautiful. Which she was right up to her death.

Her death had been another matter that the Duke refused to think about. There was no mystery there for him. He knew how and why.

How had an heir gotten past him? He had kept a close watch on the queen to make sure she had never gotten pregnant. If she had, he would have known. It's not like a woman can hide a pregnancy. Or, there was that time many years ago. Where had that chambermaid gotten off to? How could he have let her and her little bump disappear in the night? He had looked and looked for her so he could keep tabs on her. Maybe even pay her to keep quiet over time, but he had never found her or heard of a child being mysteriously born. He had thought she may have died while traveling on the road to some far away country so she could hide with her offspring.

He had threatened her and her child's life in an off-handed manner. How far away could she have traveled while with child? How was it that Captain Pellesi's daughter had found this heir with ease and he hadn't?

There was one person who would know. That would be Hurley, Captain Pellesi's first mate. He needed an audience with the man and he knew how. He also needed to finish setting this deal he had made with this man into motion.

"Lieutenant Knox, I want you to take several men to the Sea Wench and bring back Hurley. I want to question him."

"What if he doesn't come willingly?"

"Bring him any way you can. Oh, and look for someone they may be holding prisoner on board, in fact, search the ship."

"Do you want me to seize the prisoner?"

"No, you have my permission to kill them."

"As you wish."

The Duke and Hurley had made a deal. It would be just like that pirate to not honor his end of the bargain. He had agreed to take the Captain prisoner at Hurley's request. Obviously he had other plans that were to interfere with the Duke acquiring the kingdom upon the king's death. If he had to, he would put a stop to Hurley's plan and make Captain Pellesi pay for his first mate's folly.

CHAPTER 11

"Hurley!" Treea screamed once again. No answer. Where had that man gotten off to? She couldn't help but notice the advancing soldiers on horseback heading for her ship with a prisoner cart in tow. Were they coming for her now that the message had been sent to the King?

"My Lady, I can't find Hurley anywhere," said a deck hand Treea had sent in search of the first mate as soon as Treea had seen the advancing soldiers.

It was too late to pull up the plank leading to the dock as two soldiers had already set foot on it followed by the Lieutenant. Treea braced herself. She was sure they were here to take her prisoner.

The officer opened up the scroll and read its contents for all to hear. "By order of the King, we're here to take Hurley Malcomivetch into custody for questioning. You are hereby ordered to turn him over or face the consequences."

"Hurley is not here," Treea responded.

"Search the ship," ordered the Lieutenant, "and, find

the prisoner and kill them."

Treea drew her sword. "You have no right to be on my ship and you have no right to search my ship. Arm yourself!"

"You are such a fool, Lassie, but if that is what you want then so be it."

Metal hitting metal sounded aboard the deck as each hand including Treea engaged in a duel with an opponent. Each strike missing its mark but taking its toll on muscles. The Lieutenant was strong and agile but so too was Treea. She had many a fencing lesson with her Pop from the time she was ten. Then, when he had made the final decision to take her aboard the ship when her Mum died from the croup. It must have been brought on by coal dust from the fireplace, and maybe a pipe of smoke or two, he once again continued with her lessons.

The blade nearly missed her shoulder as she deflected it by spinning out of its way. She let her defenses come to her aid by jumping and ducking. This was much easier on her body than swinging her cutlass about. Tire the enemy out and then take advantage of their weakness.

Where was Hurley, she wondered? Had he left the ship without saying a word? What did the King want with him? Did they want to know what his knowledge of the heir was? How had he come across that diary in the first place? He had never said.

The Lieutenant swung almost catching her off guard while the thoughts of where and why Hurley was missing raced through her head. She had to fall backwards and roll out of the way to avoid the lieutenant's blade coming down on her neck. It was a close call. A quick scramble to her feet before he could swipe once more with his blade saved her from another attack.

Finally, the Lieutenant began to tire. She had begun to wonder if he ever would, and who had more stamina, she started to think that maybe she was the lesser foe until he faltered and she took full advantage of it.

With the swing of her blade, it made contact with the Lieutenant's side. It did not cut him enough to kill him, but he was injured. He clinched his side and began to back his way off the ship nearly losing his footing on the plank. Treea followed him in hopes of helping him find his way into the water, by kicking at the edge of the plank. Three kicks with success. The plank slipped off the edge of the ship. Down into the water went the plank and the Lieutenant. A trail of blood appeared across the water's surface indicating how badly the Lieutenant had been injured. He disappeared from sight. She hoped he had been eaten but wouldn't bet on it. Never assume your enemy is dead, most likely they escaped coming to find you in the future.

"A ghost from your past can be the death of you," her Pop always said.

Treea turned away, others needed her help. A blade clanked and skittered across the deck as one of the hands fell from a fatal wound to his abdomen. This enraged Treea. She ran at the soldier with all her might and battled him, swing for swing knocking him over the side of the ship into the cold waters below. Hopefully, he would be fish food.

One by one the soldiers were either knocked from the ship by a blow or sent in retreat to the safety of the dock which was only accessible by jumping.

"Cowards!" Treea yelled after the last soldier jumped from the ship, making it safely.

Still no sign of Hurley.

She watch while they helped the injured Lieutenant up on his horse. Just as she had thought, he was still alive. Treea was sure he would be back again on another day.

"My Lady, that was the last one." A deck hand pointed toward the last soldier who had made it successfully off the ship. "What would you have us do? Will they be back?"

"Hoist the anchor and pull the lines, we are moving a safe distance from shore."

"Aye will do."

Treea spied the door to the hold wide open. She remembered the Lieutenants orders to find and kill her prisoner. Carefully she approached the hold and looked down to see a body lying limp below. Her heart sank, hopes of using the prisoner against the King for her Pop's release were gone.

When she descended the ladder, she was surprised to see who it was that lay there in a pool of blood chained to the ship. It was not her prisoner, the heir. She wondered how he had gotten away while tears filled her eyes.

The sight before her shocked her. His blood was drained from his face. There had been no weapons seen for him to defend himself with from the attacker. Not even a dagger. He must have come down here unarmed and he had never stood a chance. A pain grew in her heart making it hard to breathe while she drew his body close to her holding his head against her chest, she stroked his hair. The skin was cold to touch. How long had he laid here in his own pool of blood?

Treea set her lips to his forehead one last time. Sobs came forth from her throat in spasms. Hurley, her love was dead. Whoever had taken her prisoner without being seen did not matter. All that mattered was how her heart felt as though it was ripped from her body. Whoever had done this was going to pay and pay dearly.

CHAPTER 12

"Mum, has anyone given you any trouble?"

"No, why? Where have you been? Your food went cold the other night and I had to feed it to the cats to keep it from spoiling. What have I told you before, if you're not coming home then tell me so I don't waste our precious food." The woman wore a tattered dress that would only take maybe one or two more times of repairing before it would be beyond help. Her beauty of her younger years lost over time. Life struggles showed in the thick lines of her brow from squinting to see the needle and thread that she so diligently worked with day in and day out.

Dale knew she would be angry with him for not returning home over the past couple of days. What would she say if she knew why? There was only one way to find out. He really needed to know anyways. What if that sea wench was right about who his father really was?

"About that Mum, please sit for a moment. I need to tell you what happened to me and ask you a question.

Please, I beg you, please tell me the truth."

She raised her brow in question but took a seat as he had asked and waited.

"I was taken captive two days ago. At first I did not know why but then I later learned from a woman who took me prisoner. Mum, she said I am the king's heir. Is this true?"

The old woman looked away causing Dale to reach out and take her hand. "Mum is this true," he repeated.

She had seemed far away in another time before she replied. "What proof does she have?"

"The woman told me about a diary she acquired and how my name was written in this book along with knowledge of my birthmark. No one knows about my birthmark beside you, Mum. Is she telling the truth? You said my Pop was a tailor."

The woman thought back to when she had been young and in love. It had been unusually cold in the castle that year. The man she loved had brought her a pair of gloves to keep her hands warm. He had told her that he had made them himself so that they would be special. In a way, this made him in her mind the beginning of a tailor, if only he had not been royalty, he would have made an excellent tailor.

"This diary, where did she get it?" His Mum asked.

"She wouldn't say. Was there such a book? Tell me the truth, please?"

"They will kill you should they find you," his Mum mumbled.

"But why? Why would they kill the only heir to the throne?"

"Because, they told me so."

"Who, Mum, who told you so?"

"Why the Duke of course. He gave me warning and I took heed and left immediately before anyone else found out. I hid with you for months on end, eating scraps thrown out by the inn in the dead of night. I foraged for food for us at night and we hid by day so no one would find us. Then, when I decided and learned that no one was looking for us in the city. And, reports were made of a woman found dead on her way to a city south of the kingdom, I thought we were safe to live the life of an ordinary town resident. That was when I felt safe for you to learn to be educated and allowed you to be schooled."

Dale sat across from his Mum at the table. He leaned back and crossed his arms. "The Duke is the one who took her Pop prisoner."

"Who's Pop is that?" His mom asked while reaching across the table in hopes of touching her son's arm in forgiveness.

"Treea Pellesi."

"Why does that name seem familiar?"

"I'm sure you have heard of Captain Pellesi?"

His mum's hand shot to her mouth. "The pirate? He has a daughter?"

"She captured me, with the intention of holding me for ransom for the release of her Pop."

"How did you get away?"

"Mum, do you remember how you always told me a man's downfall is through jealousy?"

"Aye."

"Well, that is exactly what I did. You see the first mate, he has a strong heart for Captain Pellesi's daughter and she showed an eye for me. So I took advantage of his weakness and used it against him. I merely told him I would steal his woman from him. This irked him and he challenged me to a duel, not to the death mind you, but to submission of will. The years of living among the street urchins taught me well in hand to hand combat. I overpowered him and knocked him out. Then I switched places with him and left the ship by jumping to the water. Good thing I learned to swim." The thought of swimming in the cold water brought a short chuckle from is throat. "I left in time to hear the Dukes men board the ship."

The old woman slapped her hands on the table, the gesture almost caused Dale to lose his composure. She had a way of doing that from time to time to make a point. "He sent them to kill you. You do know that right? The Duke wants you dead."

"But why would he want that Mum? It isn't even proven that I am of any importance."

"Dale, the Duke of all people knows of your importance if he knows you are still alive he will send others until you and I are dead."

"There has to be something I can do."

His mum sat silent, deep in thought. Suddenly she reached out and put her hand upon his arm. "There is only one thing you can do. You must possess that diary and take it to the king personally and make him look at it. He must read it if he is to believe that you exist. The queen died a few months ago without ever presenting him an heir of any kind. Now is the time for you to come forward, but you must be careful that the Duke does not find out that you still exist before you can prove who you are to the king. Everything that is in that diary is only known to the King or myself. When he reads it, he will know."

"Then I must get back on board Captain Pellesi's ship. That is where the diary is. Treea has it."

CHAPTER 13

Dale waited until nightfall before leaving the safety of his home. Dressing in dark clothes to help him hide in the shadows while he stole his way to the ship. But when he arrived at the dock the ship was no longer there. It had been moved to a safe distance from the shore, preventing any more attacks from the Duke's men. Now there was only one way to board the ship. He would have to swim for it and climb up the ship's flank where the chain hung from the weight of the anchor.

The cold water bit at his body. He was determined to get that book, drove himself on swimming quietly. Climbing the ships chain was difficult. His hand over hand motion went progressively well until he found the section slimed with algae growth. It was slippery and he nearly lost his hold. Quickly he brought his legs up and wrapped them about the chain, shimmying past the tricky area.

With a soft grunt, he rolled over the side of the ship and onto the deck, rolling near a canvas covered crate where he took cover briefly while a deck hand walked by while on watch. When the sailor was out of sight, Dale slipped out from underneath the cover and went in search of Treea's cabin. He had a vague idea of the layout of the ship from visiting similar ships in the past for a quick card game where he would allow the other player to win on purpose. It was his way of securing a future partner who would set him up with a wealthy female client as he had done with Hurley. In fact, he had been on this ship once before, but not for Hurley but for Captain Pellesi, who Dale had allowed to win not just one hand but two.

The captain had laughed heartily that night. "I know you let me win," he said to Dale, "I never gamble, me and card games do not belong together."

After the game, the captain had sent Dale home with a small bolt of silk fabric for his Mum as his way of thanking Dale for entertaining his pride by letting him win a couple hands of cards.

Dale never told his Mum where that bolt of silk had come from. He only told her his client had paid him well that night allowing him to afford such a luxury. In turn, she had made dresses for her clients to buy at a hefty price making her able to pay off a debt or two she had acquired over the years.

He quietly made his way about the ship in search of Treea's room. When he found it, he almost was caught by another sailor passing by on his way to take over the next watch. Dale had avoided being found by ducking into a dark alcove and holding his breath until the Sailor was well up the stairwell.

It was dark inside Treea's cabin. He had brought a small candle to use in order to search her room. But the swim to the ship had made the wick of the candle very damp and hard to light. It had taken a few tries with the flintstone before it took. Almost immediately, he found the diary sitting on the table on the other side of the room. While Treea slept in a hammock hanging from the ceiling in the middle, swaying back and forth with the motion of the ship, he crossed the room.

She looked beautiful, by the way, her hair framed her face. The sight of her made him yearn to touch her, kiss her, be with her the way they were the first night they had met. Her face showed sorrow and pain as though she were having a very troubled dream. Was she dreaming of her Pop?

Dale walked softly across the room to where the book sat. He reached out to pick it up off the table expecting to feel the cold steel on the back of his neck. The cold hard blade pressed against his skin in a warning that never came. He couldn't believe it. She never once woke.

Treea moved once in her sleep while Dale waited to make sure she did not wake before he stole away into the dark waters. His stealth he attributed to his elven heritage. Keeping in the shadows when a deck hand passed close by before he dove off the side of the boat.

Come morning when Treea awoke, she found the diary gone. She questioned every hand on deck. No one had seen or heard a thing during the night. There were only three people beside the one who had given the book to Hurley, who knew she had this book. That would have been Hurley, herself, and the heir. Since the heir was still missing and she knew for a fact that Hurley was dead there was only one possibility, maybe two. It was either the person who had given the book to Hurley or the Heir who had taken the book.

Since Hurley had died knowing who had given him the book this other unknown identity bothered her. Could they have been in cahoots with the heir all along? Maybe this was some kind of revenge against Hurley to see him find his death. He did have a few enemies that even Treea knew about. There was even a couple of the deck hands who didn't like Hurley enough to see him find his end. But, did they dislike their captain just as much?

Treea didn't think this last was such. They had always seemed pretty loyal to her Pop. Only Hurley used to try and override his orders from time to time. It was one of the causes for arguments that would break out between her and Hurley. Sometimes he wouldn't talk to her for days afterwards until he calmed down.

Not knowing if there were a traitor on deck, Treea decided it would be best that she went in search of clues to who had taken the book. And, if she could find Dale Montey if he were still alive.

She didn't give any of the hands an explanation as to why she was going ashore. Treea didn't need to. They knew she was trying to find a way to get her pop released from prison. Hurley was no longer around to do her leg work. Any one of the men would have gladly tried to help her. She only told them that they needed to stay on board and guard the ship while she was gone in search of answers and the missing prisoner.

The men grinned at her knowingly. They knew what Dale did for a living.

One of the men decided to shout a hint while she rowed the dinghy boat toward the shore. "Check the tavern where you found him last. I'm sure someone will be able to point you in the right direction."

She knew he was right. Where else would one look? It made sense to go back to the beginning. Maybe there she would learn something else useful. That was what a tavern was good for, gossip.

Outside the tavern, Treea straightened her dress and smoothed the lace about her bosom. A quick touch up of the scarf wrapped about her head allowed her large hoop earrings to hang loosely above her shoulders. Black pearls hung about her neck with a matching bracelet. Any other woman would have been overdressed. But being a pirate's daughter, this was the way Treea liked to appear. They were also gifts from her Pop.

As soon as she entered the inn, everyone, guests including knew who she was. No one could miss a pirate's daughter dressing like a pirate's daughter. Frankly, Treea didn't care if they did know. She was there on business.

A bar maid hurried over to her and looked about for a free table for this important guest. There was not one table available. The barmaid looked frantically about, "I can't seem to find you a table."

Treea waved her off. "I'm not here to eat. I'm looking for someone."

"I'm not sure if I can help you then," the barmaid replied.

"Dale, where is Dale. I know you know who I am talking about."

The barmaid's eyes went wide in astonishment. "Dale?" She looked about the room once again. "He does not seem to be here. Did you have an appointment with him?"

"No, but I want to make one. How do I do that?"

"The cost is up front, two gold pieces. I hear his price has gone up since he was last here." The barmaid grinned.

"That is robbery." Treea fished about the inside of a money pouch she had tied to her waist, even though that was less money than Hurley had paid previously. "Here, when can I expect to see him?"

CHAPTER 14

Treea couldn't wait another minute. She needed to find that book. It was her ticket to getting her Pop out of the dungeon. Sometimes you just needed to do some things by yourself.

Since most of the crew was fast asleep, Treea departed the ship, quietly taking the smallest boat that she could manage with the oars by herself. The waters were slightly choppy from the strong south wind. But, it was by the help of the wind that she was able to use the tide to bring her to shore unnoticed by any of the town's people. She was able to tie it securely to a small dock and left a gold coin for the fish merchant who kept the dock

Most of the people were still asleep or just waking. Wisps of smoke rose from chimneys of the homes of those who could afford coal.

Where was she to begin her search? Who would know Dale Montey? How shall she find him in such a large city? And, did he have the diary?

Why not start where she had first met him? The

Black Line Tavern as the deckhand had suggested while she parted the ship.

She had been there two days prior with not one sign of him. The barmaid had agreed to set up a meeting with him, telling her to give her time to find him. Treea waited those few days for the waitress to make an arrangement, hoping to meet with him in the early morning hours.

There should have been barely a soul sitting in the big room of the Tavern when she let the door creak closed behind her. The barmaid was the one who greeted her with surprisingly, no hopes of acquiring a table. She was forced to remain standing by the fire in waits of a seat.

"What can I get fer ye, young lassie?" When the table became free, the barmaid ushered her to the seat.

"I'll take a mug of your morning hot brew and a plate of eggs with fruit if you have it." Treea set a coin on the table before her. "Apples are my favorite."

"Aye, we have a few of them." She swiftly scooped up the coin and pocketed it, returning soon after with the breakfast and a hot brew."

Treea ate slowly, watching the comings and goings of the people at the Tavern. Dale was not to be seen. Could he be peering around the corner watching her, waiting for her to leave?

A crew of merchants she had never met before took over the table next to hers. She couldn't help but overhear their conversation. At first their talk was just ship talk but then it slowly became gossip of a sort. Just the mention of her Pop's name made her tune her ear carefully on to their conversation.

"Aye, did you hear that Captain Pellesi was arrested by the King's men the other day?"

"That will teach that scoundrel not to deliver rat poop to the merchants. To think that he told them it was worth two-hundred silver. They should hang him for such a shipment."

Treea's face grew red. She knew they didn't know what they were talking about. That shipment of the so-called rat poop was cocoa beans. It was a highly prized commodity in other countries.

"I heard they burned the shipment for fear that it would bring the plague down on them."

Burned? Treea couldn't believe her ears. No wonder her pop hadn't received payment for that cargo. She just thought the merchant was dragging out his payment schedule. It was funny that her pop never made an issue out of not receiving payment right away. She wondered if he knew all along that the cocoa had been burned. Even Hurley never mentioned a thing about the fate of the cargo.

"I'm glad they arrested him. I hope it sends a strong message to anyone else who wants to try to con the King into thinking that garbage is a prized commodity."

All the talk got to Treea. She couldn't take it anymore. She just so happened to have a small bag of the so-called rat poop on her. With a quick yank of its strings, she had the pouch off her waist sash and open. Taking a small handful of the so described beans from it and placed them down on the table before the men. "That rat poop, was cocoa beans. Put one in your mouth like this," she demonstrated, "and suck on it. It is a delicacy. They make hot chocolate from it. It is the drink of the Gods in the other lands."

One of the men raised his hand ready to swipe the rat poop off his table. Treea put her hand in the way, stopping him. Dale scoffed up a bean from behind Treea's hand and popped it into his mouth to the horror of the men sitting at the table. She had been so upset by the talk of the cocoa beans she had never seen Dale come into the tavern.

"You should know," Dale said with the bean pocketed in the side of his mouth, "that the beans do have an aphrodisiac effect. You want more sex with your women, then feed them handfuls of these."

One by one, each of the men at the table took a bean and placed it in their mouths. If Dale hadn't been there to show it was edible, then they would never have believed a word Treea had said. Instead, they would have continued to scoff at her, not only because she was a woman, but also because she was the daughter of the imprisoned pirate Captain Pellesi. Each of the men's faces responded to the taste of the beans, surprised to learn that what was thought to be rat poop was not that.

"You know about cocoa beans?" Treea asked, surprised by Dale's sudden interest.

He laughed. "I've used them many times. Most often I can only acquire them through the black market, which is where I think your beans were initially headed to before the Duke got a hold of the shipment."

"How is it that you know of our shipment?"

"The Captain told me about it. He was - is - a friend, acquaintance of mine."

"He was falsely imprisoned." Treea responded. "I need to find a way to make the king release him. There is no reason for him to be arrested."

The men looked about them for answers agreeing with her that there must be a way to rectify his arrest. "Maybe if we each go to the king and vouch for him and tell the king that the shipment wasn't rat poop as was suspected." Each man continued to toss ideas out into the open, but none that could be agreed on. The fact that they would have to face the Duke first put a damper on any formidable plan. Not one of the men dared to face the Duke.

"We will find a way. Come with me." Dale took Treea by the hand and led her away, up the stairs and down the hallway, out the doorway into a back alley. Nightfall hid their movement. How long had she been at the tavern trying to form some kind of plan to rescue her Pop?

Treea did not question Dale when he led her away. She was happy that she had found him, even if she has wasted a few too many coins on him. She could take him prisoner once again or she could allow him to find a different approach to the King and freeing her pop. She was sure he had to have the diary. Maybe he already had a plan too.

They wove their way through the back alleyways until they came to stop before a rotten plank door. It led up two flights of stairs above a tailor shop. Treea took in the sight of the hard living conditions. Two wooden chairs accompanied a makeshift table made out of an old stump and a small plank of wood. The beds were of straw and old ratty blankets. An old woman was sound asleep in one of the beds.

Dale put a finger to his lips. She knew he didn't want her to wake the sleeping woman.

A dark woolen cloth was wrapped about an object on the table. He snatched it up and led Treea back out into the alleyway, into the dark of the night. "I know where we can go," he said. Taking her back to the tavern, they did not enter, but instead entered the stable that only held the riderless horses of the tavern's guests who were spending the night. Another doorway inside led to the basement where the grain was stored. "No one will bother us in here."

Treea's hand touched the hilt of her short sword. There was no one here to stop her from capturing him. The thought of butchering him the way Hurley had been butchered did cross her mind and would've gladly have done so if she didn't need him as her prisoner.

Dale didn't wait for Treea to question why they were in the basement. He found a sack of grain and took a seat upon it after lighting a candle that set on a wooden crate. He broke their silence aware of the glint of steel hanging from her sash. "You sent a message to the King about my existence, didn't you?"

"I did. I told him you were my prisoner."

"Well, that was an ill thought out plan on your part."

Treea prepared to pull her sword from its sheath. "It was not. It was a perfectly thought out plan."

"Did it work?"

"Not yet. It is too soon for the King to respond."

Dale chuckled.

"What's so funny?"

"You..."

"Me?"

"Yes, you. You are so naive to think that such a plan would work at all."

"Only naive to let someone else keep watch over my prisoner. How is it that you killed Hurley anyways?"

Dale slipped a hand before his collar and unbuttoned his shirt to expose a glimpse of his chest. Treea expected him to pull a knife out from under his shirt, maybe a throwing dagger perhaps. He procured none. Instead, he lazily rested his back against the wall and eyed her.

"I merely took advantage of his jealously. I only knocked him out. I did not kill him."

Her brows furrowed in anger. "You left him to die." She spat at him.

"Had I stayed in your hold, not only would your beloved Hurley been dead, I would have been dead too. You would have nothing."

"The King's men wouldn't have killed you. They were there to rescue you."

"You are more naive than I thought. You don't know a thing about the Duke, do you? He was the one who sent the guards after you and your ship. They were not there to rescue me. They were there to kill me."

"Why would they want to kill you if you are the King's heir? That doesn't make any sense."

"The Duke doesn't want our king to have an heir. He is next in line to the throne as long as I stay out of the picture."

"How do you know this?"

"Because he is the one who ordered to have my mother killed while she was with child."

"But wasn't that to save the King from embarrassment of having an illegitimate child?"

"No, the king loved my mother and she loved him. They would be married if it hadn't been for the Duke's interference. She ran to save her life. She ran to save the life of her unborn child."

"If that is the case, what do you plan to do? The king knows you exist."

"I know that the Duke knows I exist. I'm not so sure about the King. Your ransom note may have never reached the king. The duke may have intercepted it and then ordered the strike on your ship."

"That still hasn't answered my question." Treea let her hand slip off the hilt of her sword.

"Come sit beside me and let's talk about this more." Dale patted the sack he sat on, beckoning Treea to join him.

She obliged. She had been standing long enough. Her feet were killing her in the boots she wore. When her arm brushed against Dale, she found him warm. Her teeth had begun to chatter from the cellar's dampness.

"Are you cold?" Dale wrapped his arm about her and pulled her closer to him.

His touch sent a tingle deep inside her. There was no reason she should feel such a thing. Her feelings had been for Hurley. Even though he was gone, it was too soon to begin thinking about someone else in that manner. She wanted to pull away to make that feeling stop, but she was cold and he was warm. She relented and allowed herself to be drawn against his body.

"If the king doesn't know you exist and the duke wants you dead, then how am I going to get my pop back?"

"I'm going to need an audience with the king. Somehow, some way, I need to prove to him that I am his long lost son. The child he never knew existed. Then and only then, I may be able to convince him that the arrest of your pop was a terrible mistake and misunderstanding. If he sees it my way, he will release him immediately."

"But what about the Duke?"

Dale began to stroke his fingers up and down Treea's arm, reigniting the tingling inside her. It started in her stomach and traveled to her inner thighs. She found herself gazing into his eyes while he spoke."

"He will pose a problem if I can't get to the king before he intervenes. I could be arrested and ordered executed for impersonating a royalist." His lips moved closer to her. Suddenly, they were making contact with her neck below her earlobe, which his tongue touched in soft strokes that caused her to gasp unexpectedly. He stopped as suddenly as he started.

Treea wanted more but said nothing of the sort. "How do you plan to get past the Duke?" She turned her face more so that she could look into his eyes easier. It would be so easy for her to melt into his arms. Her lips were inches away from his.

"I will need someone to distract the duke for me." His lips were almost touching hers.

"Do you want me to distract him for you?" She leaned closer to him making their lips touch, kissing him eagerly. Hurley was dead, but that wouldn't make the arousal go away. Dale was alive and it was his lips that were touching hers.

Dale turned to accommodate their positions, pushing her backwards on the grain sack. His hands cradled her face gently. Slowly one hand crept toward her chest where he found the strings to undo the lacing letting her breast pop out of their binding. His lips found her nipples, sucking them gently and stroking the tips with his tongue.

Treea couldn't help but gasp at the growing arousal. She wanted to shed her dress and feel his skin against hers. Instead, he pushed up the hem of her dress exposing her lower abdomen and kissed her below her button, following a straight path to her patch. Her legs twitched with the need to spread, but his body was in their way.

Instead, he stood, taking her by the hand he pulled her to her feet and spun her around, pushing her breast up against the wall. The cold cooled her heat for only a short moment which ended when he once again hiked up her hem after unhitching his own pants. His hand stroked her ass gently. He bent over and kissed it tenderly following a path to the inside of her thigh.

This time she was able to spread her legs. His fingers found her love spot and stroked it tenderly. "Your beginning to warm up."

Treea had a hard time talking. She panted in between words. "I'm not cold anymore."

"Do you want me to stop? I can stop if you want me too."

"No, please don't stop."

"You want some more?" He said softly in her ear.

"Yes, I want more."

Dale kissed her neck. He grinned. "Would you beg for more if I stopped?" He started to pull away. Still holding the hem of her dress up against her back.

Treea hissed. "Don't stop now. You can't leave me like this. You have to, please don't stop."

Dale rubbed his hand over her ass again. With one swift jerk, his shaft was in her. There was no turning back. He pumped against her driving deeper and deeper inside. She pushed against him in rhythm with every thrust. Her ass arched upward in desire until she couldn't hold herself back anymore. He went deep as he could go coming the same time as she did. He wrapped his arms around her and held her tightly against him until his convulsions stopped.

He released her and reclined back on the grain sack. Treea giggled and let herself fall on top of him. "I want more." She said chasing his lips to kiss him.

Dale laughed. "I'll tell you what. I'll give you lots more where that came from if you distract the duke for me."

Treea smiled in return. "All right. You have a deal. But you might not like how I plan to divert him."

Dale raised an eyebrow. "What's that supposed to mean?"

"Ha, a girl has to do what a girl has to do."

"If only it was that easy," Dale replied.

CHAPTER 15

Treea didn't know what had gotten into her last night. How could she jump from the arms of one man who was now dead into the arms of another, one she didn't even know. But it felt so right to be in those arms. Hurley hadn't even been dead for more than a couple of days. Had she not loved him more than she thought she had? She would never know if his feelings for her were more than he had ever let on to, especially after the way he had reacted to her encounter with the heir.

She would miss Hurley dearly, but after how she had behaved with Dale last night she began to question as to whether she had really been in love with Hurley the way she thought she'd been. They did have many a spat that her Pop had to break up over some stupid thing as in how she dressed by wearing men's pants instead of dresses. Treea kept telling him the sea wind was too cold for her to be wearing a dress. Their argument would always end with her yelling at him, "Why don't you trying wearing a dress for a day with that sea wind so your balls will freeze and fall off!"

She did not miss the fights they had.

Dale was different. He was gentle, younger, and much better looking than Hurley. But that was not a good reason to become involved with him. If things went right, Dale would become the King's rightful heir and her Pop would be released. They would return to the sea and probably never return to this kingdom ever again. Which would mean that Treea would never see Dale ever again and he would go on to marry some princess from a far away land as the King had done. Should this even matter to her? There was many a man on the sea.

All this did not help to change how her feelings for Dale had begun to grow. How she couldn't stop thinking about him. She never once had this problem with Hurley.

"You be careful of the Duke," Treea said before leaving Dale in the cellar hole. They had hid there until the early morning dawn, slipping away while the city still slept.

"Aye, and you too, my Lady. I do know a bit more about taking care of myself in predicaments than you would care to know. I will see to it that your Pop is released soon." Dale said while he kissed her hand tenderly before letting it go.

Once she was gone and out of sight, Dale made his way through the winding streets of the city. He had to travel across the town. The King's castle was to the South at the top of a craggy cliff where the King could look down at his town's people from the top of the torrents. Here the castle was safe from crashing sea waves when a storm brewed. The sea water never reaching the top of the cliff wall.

A dense forest separated the Castle from the town. Miles and miles of forest on each side held wildlife that could be hunted for an extra fee and a license from the king. Not many could afford the license and some poaching did occur. First offense if caught was a fine of double the amount of the license fee. Second offense was prison. Third offense was indentured as a servant for the rest of the life of the offender. Rarely did anyone ever escape the services of the castle as his mother did.

How she came to be a servant at the castle was not known to Dale. He never knew she had anything to do with the castle up until recently. If he had taken the time to read her diary, he had in his possession he would have had a small glimpse of her life. He might even have learned how she had come to be indentured to the castle. Diaries were a private matter and it was his mother's private matter and not to be looked into by him unless it would help his matters.

Dale not only loved his Mum, but he respected her. He never told her what he was doing for a living while trying to pay his way through college. Herbalism and alchemy was a hard thing to learn. He had learned some stuff, but he had only begun his lessons this past year. There were a good many more years to go before he was to move past the apprentice stage.

Thinking of this reminded him of how he had not mentioned his nonappearance to his master. The master only waved him off and told him to see him after he was done taking care of his matters. Never once did the man question him as to where he had gotten off to. Dale had to wonder if his master knew all along about him. The wise man had a tendency to know things no one else seemed to know.

Before leaving the city, Dale had stopped to check up on his Mum one last time. He had to make sure she was still safe. Which she was. But by his stopping in and showing her the book she made him change into his finest. She didn't want the King seeing his only son in rags.

Loose wool pants and leather boots accompanied a white cotton button down shirt with a red wrap headband pinning his hair away from his face. It also hid the points to his ears. His Mum finished him off with a wool cape pinned at the neck by a brooch. It had been given to her by the King's son, who was Dale's father, as a token of his love. He even told her that it might come in handy someday, possibly saving her life. It was an heirloom of some sort.

When she was done with him, he was spun before the only mirror they owned so he could see his transformation. He certainly looked dashing. "Whatever you do, don't ruin those clothes. It will be years before I can make you another one of those shirts."

Dale laughed. "Mum, if the King accepts me as his heir I will have many of these shirts."

She put her hand against his cheek which he took hold of and brought it to his lips to lay a tender kiss upon. "But those will not be made by me."

"Nay, they wouldn't be unless you insisted upon making them."

His comment brought a smile to her face.

It was a long walk to the castle. He had to travel on foot. Horses were not cheap and carriages were even more costly.

Along the way, he found a knotty stout branch to use for a walking stick. It also would do well as a staff if he needed to defend himself if need be. When one does not plan for trouble, trouble always finds you.

The castle was a good day's walk. He arrived at the gate just before sundown. If he were lucky, he might be given an audience by the King today.

"You there, state your business."

"I wish for an audience with the King."

A guard stepped forward to give Dale further

inspection and turned to his fellow mates guarding the entrance. "He wears the Baron's brooch."

"Let him pass." A tall man in light mail answered. He appeared to be a captain of the troupe. "Escort him to the King's Hall."

It seemed too simple, using the brooch as a way into the castle.

Dale remained silent while he followed the guard into the castle. When they reached the hall, he was told to stay and wait while the King was told he had company. A couple of times the guard addressed Dale by calling him, "My Lord." Never once did he expect to be mistaken for a Baron.

While he waited, a tray of tea and cakes were delivered by a maid and set upon a table near by. Dale did not touch these. He had been brought up proper by his Mum. The King needed to invite you if you were to dine with him.

"What may I do for you?"

Dale had his back to the speaker. He had been busy admiring a cloth hanging upon the wall. The tapestry was that of the layout of the streets of the town where Dale had come from. When he heard a voice, he turned around upon his heel to lay eyes upon the King for the first time in his life. Was he supposed to kneel or bow? Dale picked bow.

"Your majesty." Dale did not know how to begin. He had tried to rehearse while traveling here just exactly what he would say to the King about his mother but now the words fell short from his lips. Especially when he saw the duke was standing behind the King. There was something about the man that made Dale pause before speaking. Was it the way the Duke narrowed his eyes at him or the fact that the man stood watch over the King? Dale couldn't quite put his finger on it.

The King was one step ahead of Dale. He was tipped off by the brooch. There was only one person who would have had that brooch. When he saw it, the memories of her came flooding back. "I know this brooch. I gave it to someone many years ago."

Dale smiled. "It is my mother's."

The Duke stepped forward. "Your mother? How do you know it belonged to your mother? I heard she died when you were a babe."

This called for a careful approach. Dale knew the Duke wanted the heir dead for some unknown reason. He knew he couldn't trust him. What the man was up to and what would happen once the King left Dale's presence was without question. He had already tried once to kill him. Most likely he would try again, somehow, some way.

"My Mum is alive and healthy."

"Then the brooch was attached to your blanket and your adoptive mother gave it to you." The Duke responded. Not once did the Duke look to the King for approval. He continued to stare Dale down.

"No, I was not adopted. My birth mother still lives."

Dale could not help but notice how the Duke balled his fists at the news of his mother's good health and long life. Now he focused his attention on the King. "Your majesty, I brought you the book my mother kept while she was living here in the castle as a young woman. It may shed some light to what happened to her and how I came to be." He retrieved the book from inside his cloak while he spoke and held it out to the King to take.

The Duke started to reach for the book before the King, but his hand was swatted away by Dale allowing the King to receive the book himself.

"How dare you?" reacted the Duke.

"Ellington, leave us." The King waved him away with his free hand.

This got Dale a sneer from the Duke before leaving the two of them alone.

"Come sit with me, son, and have some tea and cakes while I look at this here book of yours."

Dale sat across from the King at the small oval table and sipped tea and nibbled on cakes while he waited for comment from the King while he read the book. A few times the King's face become flush from reading certain passages and even looked up once to ask, "Did you read any of this book?"

"Nay," Dale answered. "Those are my mother's private thoughts. I will only read them if necessary."

"Then how did you know what was written in this here book? And, weren't you captured and being held captive by some Pirate's daughter?"

"I escaped. A friend, the very woman who kidnapped me, told me about what was written in the book."

"You call this woman who held you captive for ransom of her Pirate father a friend?"

"Aye, she never meant me any harm. She was just looking for a way to get her father given back to her. She is not a terrible person. He, like my Mum, is the only family she has got."

The King seemed to study Dale before reading on until he came to another passage. "You have your mother's eyes. Do you have this so called birthmark?"

"You want me to show it to you? It is a private mark."

"If you are my son as this indicates and had I known, I'm sure I would have seen it when you were a babe. Show me the mark as proof to match the book."

Dale's face turned a bright shade of pink. He never once thought he would be doing this before the King of all people, even if he were supposed to be his father. "All right." He stood up and hitched up his shirt and dropped his pants. The dark colored birthmark covered one testicle and part of his manhood.

"You are marked like a bull and built like one too, Son," The King emphasized the word son while he laughed at the sight.

Dale quickly recovered his composer by hitching his pants back up.

The two sat speechless for a few moments before the King finally spoke after a long sip of his tea. "All this time I did not know I had a son. You will have to move into the castle at once. There is a lot of work to be done and a lot for you to learn before you will take over the reins of the Kingdom. I thought for sure I would be forced to hand down the crown to Duke Ellington. Now, I'm glad to hear I have a better alternative. If you are anything like your mother, then you are the right choice to be my heir. We must send for your mother at once. I have missed her all these years. It's a wonderful surprise to know she is still alive after all this time."

"I'm not sure she will come."

"Is she still mad at me after all these years?"

"Nay, it's that she still fears for her life."

"But why? I can protect her. I can protect her more if she is by my side."

Dale wasn't sure if the King knew who wanted he and his mother dead. Even Dale wasn't sure. Treea seemed to believe they were in danger from the Duke. If the Duke had been expecting to be the heir to the throne then, that would explain why he had been the one to order the soldiers to kill Treea's prisoner. He had to keep his mother safe and the only way was to keep her whereabouts hidden until the truth of the matter was dealt with by the King.

"She is safe for now. I will be happy to send for her when I am sure all the danger is gone."

"Well, then Son, we will have to come to the bottom of these threats and find out who is threatening her. Won't we?"

"Aye, I plan on seeing to that."

CHAPTER 16

Duke Ellington's hair felt as though it stood up on end when he laid eyes on the King's visitor. Then to learn that he was the one who was claiming to be the King's heir set him on flame. His soldiers told him they had killed the prisoner. They were supposed to find Hurley. But they never did. In fact, the man had not turned up yet. Had he double-crossed the Duke?

There was only one thing to do to a Pirate to get even with them when they double-crossed you. Set their ship on fire. He paid his lieutenant a visit.

"Lieutenant Knox, any word on the whereabouts of Hurley?"

"Nay, Sire, he has not yet turned up."

"I want you and your men to set the Sea Wench on fire."

"Aye, Sire, if that is what you wish. Consider it done."

"Oh, and make sure that the daughter of the Pirate Pellesi is dead. She has caused me enough trouble."

The lieutenant bowed and left hurrying away.

There was no way the Duke would be able to change the King's mind once he decided to make the illegitimate heir his successor. He would just have to take matters into his own hands again. He had managed to keep the Queen from bearing an offspring. He even managed to kill her, slowly, of course. Now he would have to take care of this new threat to the crown. Maybe a slow working poison would suffice or maybe he could be sent out to a mock battle and have him killed by accident. The accident would be a better choice.

Better yet a celebratory duel for the hand of a fair maiden. He had a change of plans for the lieutenant and quickly found him preparing with his men outside the barracks.

"Good, I found you in time. I've had a change of heart. Instead of killing that Pirate's daughter I have a better idea. She would make a lovely prize wouldn't she?"

Knox didn't know how to respond. "She is a beauty." Agreeing was always the best policy when it came to politics.

"Wouldn't you love to win her in a jousting battle?"

"Jousting? Aye, she would make a mighty fine prize for a jousting battle."

Duke Ellington smiled. He knew the lieutenant was the best jouster in the kingdom. She would be an easy win for him and the most successful in making the heir's death appear to be accidental should he see fit to take part in the contest. Most likely he would since he referred to her as being a friend. "Bring her back alive. We will keep her in my tower until the day of the Joust. We will hold a fair that day and celebrate a day for our King. Oh, and Knox, don't worry, I will post your entry fee. You are my champion and deserve this woman."

"Thank you, Sire." The lieutenant bowed.

The Duke left the officer to his work and watched for a short time while Knox barked out orders to his men on how and what they were to set out to do. The day was turning out better than he had expected.

CHAPTER 17

Treea made it back to the ship while the crew slept. She walked about the deck pondering on how she was going to distract the duke while Dale set his plan in motion for the next few days. Nothing she came up with seemed to appease her. Would she be able to bring herself to do that which she had implied to Dale before they parted? Could she really seduce the Duke?

The actual seducer appeared to be Dale, but it did go with his line of work. It was shady, but who was she to judge, wasn't she a pirate's daughter?

Maybe she should just pay the Duke a personal visit and take a gamble. Dale should be at the castle by now. Hopefully, he hadn't been imprisoned. All hope would be lost if that happened.

"My Lady, a ship approaches from our South." The crew hand yelled from the Crow's nest above. "It is coming straight for us."

"Does it bear a flag?"

"Aye, it does. It's the Duke's colors."

"Ring the alarm! I don't trust this ship. They tried to board us once already, they may try once again." Treea shaded her eyes trying to see off in the distance. She needed a scope, like the one the sailor used up in the nest. She had sent him up there at sunrise, it was a quirk of a feeling that something bad might happen. This was not the way she had planned on paying the Duke his visit.

A bell on the deck was rung by another sailor calling everyone to arm themselves. Twenty sailors joined Treea on deck, waiting for the ship to approach.

It wasn't a fast moving vessel. They could've easily outrun it if they were willing to set sail back out to the open seas. This was not their intent. Instead, they would stand their ground and fight if need be.

The ship came closer. Treea could barely make out the shape of the vessel, but the sailor with the scope could see it better. "My Lady, the ship is armed with cannons," he shouted down to her.

The man, who was fifteen years senior to Treea took the helm, "Do you want us to out run it?"

Too late to run. Archers appeared on the Duke's ship and began launching flaming arrows. Treea had never taken flaming arrows into account. The crew ran about trying to put the fires out, but the arrows kept coming in massive volleys.

The helm man tried to have the anchor hoisted, but it was too late to try to run. Their ship was aflame and the only thing to do was to jump into the water or onto the other ship, which is what they all chose to do once the ship was close enough.

By using the ropes to the sails, they were able to swing from the flaming ship to the Duke's ship with ease. Any cargo they had was about to be lost. Thankfully, they had nothing of great value on board. They had taken care of that load the day Captain Pellesi was taken prisoner.

As soon as they set foot on the Duke's ship, archers dropped their bows and produced short swords to defend themselves with. Each man engaged in combat while the Sea Wench burned. Smoke filled the air making it hard to see the enemy or the fellow crew members. Clanging swords rang out along with shouts while the fighting continued.

Treea knocked her opponent down and prepared to take on the next soldier when an arm grabbed her about the neck from behind, choking off her air flow. She tried with all her might to fight off her attacker before she lost conscious from the lack of air in her lungs. Before she passed out, she thought of Dale and wondered if this was it. Was she about to join Hurley in the after world?

CHAPTER 18

Duke Ellington was surprised to learn the King had sprung into action as fast as he did with this supposed heir to the throne. How could he be so certain that this was not an impostor? Though, the duke was certain it wasn't either. The resemblance to the king was there. Between his eyes and his hair right down to the stature of his body if compared to how the King had looked in his younger years.

This was why he had sought out the Lieutenant to capture Pellesi's daughter. Which he had learned just in the nick of time, had happened. Things were finally going as the Duke had planned. He was even able to be present when the King announced the date the coronation was to take place.

"Your majesty, may I make an announcement to go along with the Coronation?"

"Aye, Ellington. What is it that you wish to say?"

"I would like to arrange a celebration of honor your son. It would also have an event that would bring a substantial amount of gold to your coffer. A contest of a sort, for the hand of a maiden. Not so much a duel of swords but more of a jousting match."

"What an excellent idea, Ellington. You have a maiden to spare?" The king knew the Duke kept a large collection of women about his compound. It was rarely that he would let them out of his service. "I am honored that you would do such a thing for my son."

"Indeed - I will go make the arrangements then."

The duke wanted to jump for joy when the king agreed to the contest. At first he thought that maybe, the King wouldn't accept his offer, by the way, he had appeared to have a skeptical eyebrow raised when he made his suggestion. Miracles do happen and so do accidents.

Plans were made, posters were placed about the streets of the city and in surrounding towns. A fair was to take place outside the King's city just beyond the forest. Tents were set up to house contestants traveling from far away.

News of jousting matches traveled fast when not only a purse was offered, but also a maiden too. Many times the winner also was able to claim a high ranking spot in the King's army. That meant, secure employment and money to send back home to support their family. It also meant possible death.

The city was bustling with its own activity while vendors arranged to set up a market area outside the city gates near where the jousting match was to take place. It had been years since the city had such an advent that would bring income to its citizens.

Duke Ellington had sought out his Lieutenant before the match was to begin. "Is our prize in top condition?"

"Aye, and she is such a lovely lassie at that. I never truly knew she was such a beauty until the maids drew her bath for her. It certainly did wonders for her. I want to thank you for arranging this match. I look forward to my new mistress." A broad proud grin covered the Lieutenant's face. All the bets were for him to win.

Ellington snickered at the Lieutenant's arrogance. "I see you do have quite the competition. That one over there," he pointed to a man built like a boulder. "He is going to be tough to beat because of his size, but if you look closely, you will see a small flaw in his armor just below his breastplate. If you sink your lance there, you should be able to easily unseat him."

The Lieutenant smirked at the Duke's advice. "Aye, thank you for looking out for me, but as a trained guard, I know how to look for my opponents weaknesses. The only one I am worried about is the heir I am supposed to go up against if your plan goes as expected. I have not seen his armor yet. He is thin but built like that of a street thug. If I do not kill him when I unseat him, the going will be tough in the hand to hand combat. But I do like a challenge."

"My guess, is that he can't even ride. His control over his horse will be something to see." The duke replied while he scanned the growing crowd for the arrival of the King and his heir.

"Where is our pretty little prize anyways? I would like to take one last look at her before you carry her away."

At the edge of the forest in a tent set off by itself was where the Lieutenant led the duke. It was heavily guarded. They didn't need someone stealing the prize before the competition took place, nor did they need the prize escaping which was the more likely thing to happen.

Her hair was done up in a fashion worn by royalty as the duke had requested. The gown was that of satin with a velvet sash about the waist. Lace covered her bodice exposing a deep cleavage.

This was his first face to face meeting with the famous pirate's daughter. She had her father's eyes that met his with a bold, cunning look of a pirate. He knew her spirit burned deep. Such a fiery lassie, she should have been added to his own collection. He would make her surrender to him while in chains.

"You're such a lovely one." Ellington lifted a loose strand of hair off Treea's neck with a single finger. Then with that same finger he gently stroked her neck from her ear down to her bare shoulder.

Treea had many ideas floating around in her head. She was supposed to distract the duke from discovering Dale, but that had never happened as planned. From the look of the events taking place, he never needed her help to begin with. Now she was a ploy in some scheme the duke had cooked up at her convenience.

Was he doing this to her to get back at her for discovering the heir's existence? Or, was there some other plan he had in the works to stop the King's plans of Dale's coronation. The girls in the compound had been buzzing about it for the past few weeks while they worked on Treea's appearance.

With a tweak to her hair and a scrubbing in the tub, even she could see her own transformation. The dress she wore was the most beautiful dress she had ever seen. It was something she had never dreamed she would have worn, let alone enjoyed wearing since she didn't like dresses.

Except when it came to Dale. He had made that dress worth while wearing. She had never stopped thinking about that night in the cellar hole. His touch still lingered after weeks had gone by.

All this was also complicating things for having her Pop released from his bonds. The fire that burned in her eyes was not a heat from her loins, but the anger she felt for the Duke. "You will pay for this." What else was she to say?

Ellington laughed. "Such a fiery wench. Such words make me want to take you before the contest to try you out. But I don't want to mess up your beautiful dress or your lovely hair. The servants put such great effort in making you presentable for this day."

He did move about her while he spoke to stop and stand behind her. He wrapped his arms about her waist and pulled her close to him to whisper in her ear. "I will buy a visit from the winner, I promise." His hands slide to her breast while his fingers sought out her nipples and gave them a brief pinch before letting her go.

It took all of Treea's will to keep from kicking him where he deserved it the most. His touch left her defiled.

"My Lord, the games are about to begin." Announced a messenger sent by the King to find the Duke.

"Aye, let the fun begin." Ellington winked at Treea as he departed the tent with the messenger.

CHAPTER 19

"Welcome all to the Coronation of Dale Montey, the King's long lost son." The announcer began, "We have a series of jousting matches planned for today to entertain the King and Prince. All who wish to enter, need to see John Marvich with an entry fee." A cheer rose from the gathered crowd at the edge of the arena.

"The prize is a purse of 100 gold pieces that will make any contestant happy to win, along with the hand of this fair maiden." The announcer pulled Treea by the arm with the help of another to display her to the crowd of contestants and viewers.

The sight of Treea sucked the air out of Dale's lungs. For weeks since he had met with the king, he had worried about her. He had not caught sight of her once. She had promised to distract the duke from the King's presence, but she had never arrived at the castle.

He thought she had either chickened out or something bad had happened to her. The later being his final conclusion when he had learned of the Sea Wench's fate days after his arrival at the castle.

He had kept his word about requesting the King release her pop from prison. The king had the papers drawn up hours ago. By the end of the day, her pop should be a free man. Now though, he would be a pirate without a ship. His daughter held captive, to be given as a prize.

Dale couldn't help but reach out and grab onto the King's wrist with a start at the sight of Treea. "That's her. Captain Pellesi's daughter. She didn't burn with the ship as was reported. He has had her captive."

The King furrowed his brow. It was too late to take matters in his own hands and stop the match. The entry fees had already been accepted. If he stopped the contest over the matter of the women, the crowd would be in an uproar. It wasn't something that should be done.

"I can't do anything in my power to stop this."

What was Dale to do? He couldn't let Treea be treated like this. She didn't deserve to be a slave mistress. This had to stop. What if?

"I want to enter," Dale announced.

"You what?" The duke interjected from the other side of the King. He had to fight the smile from appearing on his face when he heard Dale's announcement.

"I want to enter the contest," Dale repeated loud enough for everyone to hear, including Treea.

"I forbid it," The King replied, "It is too dangerous. There are other women out there that are more beautiful than she is."

"I don't want another woman. All I want is her." Dale stated loudly.

A cheer erupted from the crowd. It was almost unheard of for a prince to enter into a jousting contest. "You could let someone stand in for him," suggested the Duke. Not what he had planned for, but to see Dale loose the woman he wanted was enjoyable just he same. There were other ways to cause the new prince to accidently die.

"Aye, that is a grand idea. I know just the one to be his challenger. The king turned behind him and called for his messenger. He carefully whispered his request into the messenger's ear. Even Dale didn't hear whom the King requested to be as his challenger." All he knew was that the messenger wasted no time. He ran off in the direction of the castle.

"So, are you going to divulge who the challenger will be or are you going to make us wait to see?" asked the Duke. Curiosity buzzed about the grounds.

The king stood to make his announcement. "As many of you know, Captain Pellesi has been held as a prisoner in the tower for months. I have decided to have him released on the condition that he is to be the challenger for my son since she," the King pointed toward Treea. "She is his daughter. How grand an event. I think this has just raised the stakes even higher. Don't you Duke Ellington?"

Ellington was appalled and surprised at the same time. The captain would be more than an acceptable match for the Lieutenant. But the captain would have a stronger motive to win than any of the other contestants. It was his daughter.

The duke couldn't decline the challenge. The contest had to go on. "Aye, your majesty, this will be the jousting match of the century."

CHAPTER 20

The messenger handed the sealed scroll to the guard outside the tower's prison gate. After carefully breaking the seal, the guard read it and nodded in acknowledgement.

"You there," the guard called out to a passing fellow guard. "You are to fetch Captain Pellesi and go with the messenger to see the King. The captain has been entered into the jousting match."

"What for? Since when are prisoners allowed to enter the matches?"

"See for yourself." The guard opened the message. "Says so by the King."

"I don't see why he can." The guard huffed while he stormed off to the captain's cell. The messenger was close behind him.

"The captain's daughter is one of the prizes of the match." The messenger explained.

The guard stopped in his tracks. "You don't say? Why do I always have to miss the best events?" They continued down a flight of stair to the basement of the tower.

"Hey, Pellesi, the king is granting you a request. If I were you, I would take the offer."

The door swung open with a creak of rusty hinges. The torch on the wall exposed the captain living in deplorable conditions. His cell stank of urine and feces along with the odor of a man who had not bathed in weeks.

"He has kept me prisoner for months on a bogus charge and now he request my services?" Captain Pellesi spat his distrust at the guard's feet.

"Well, if you really feel that way, you don't have to accept it. You can remain right where you are. It is only a jousting match and he needs a challenger for the prince."

"Prince, what prince? And what is in it for me beside money I can't spend while rotting in my cell?"

"New has it, that this prince was discovered recently. I hear he is some sort of long lost son that he never knew existed. I say it is bogus, but I don't know what proof the man has besides some brooch and a book. Supposedly he was found by none other than your daughter."

This news got Captain Pellesi's attention. "My daughter, what say of her?"

The guard showed the captain the message from the king. "So what does that have to do with my needing to accept the challenge?"

The messenger spoke up while they climbed the stair. "Captain, one of the prizes of the contest is your daughter. She is being offered along with a purse of gold by none other than Duke Ellington."

"Does that answer your question?" asked the guard.

Captain Pellesi winced at the answer to his question. Of course, they would make sure he would compete. How else to secure this than by using his daughter as the stake. He would never be able to turn down the chance to save his daughter from the hands of the duke.

CHAPTER 21

Ellington's plans were amiss. Things were not going as he had planned. The king was supposed to allow this heir to compete in the jousting match. How else was he supposed to die an accidental death?

Now he would have to come up with another plan.

"Your majesty, does your son like the hunt?" the duke inquired.

"I don't know. Son, do you like hunting?"

Dale was not sure if this was a trick question. Maybe the Duke was hoping for him to incriminate himself by saying how he had hunted all the time. Maybe the duke also knew this and had inside information that he had hunted for years without acquiring a permit. How should he answer this?

"I'm not sure," Dale replied with a little white lie.

"I think Ellington is planning a hunt soon."

"Aye, I am, your majesty. Would the prince like to accompany me?" Ellington leaned forward to get a better glimpse of Dale's face when he replied. "I would love for you to join me and I can share my knowledge and skill of hunting. It is the most I can do for my majesty's son."

"That is so kind of you, Ellington." The king turned back to Dale. "What do you say, son? Ellington is a good shot with a bow."

"Maybe someday in the future. There is too much to learn in the coming months for me to worry about a hunting expedition. But, thank you for your offer." Dale said graciously. The last thing he wanted was to be on a hunt with the Duke. One of them was not going to come back alive, Dale was sure of that.

"Oh boo. Well, if you ever change your mind, just say so and we will ride together."

Trumpets announced the first two contestants. Neither of which were from this kingdom. One was the burly man that the duke had pointed out to the Lieutenant earlier. The other one brought laughter from the crowd.

He was a small man, who stood no taller than an ordinary man's waist. His horse was too big for his body. Ponies were not allowed in the contest. All contestants were to sit on horses of the same height out of fairness.

The king leaned forward with interest. "Is that a dwarf?"

"Aye, that he is. It seems that there are many coming from your surround lands to pay homage to your new heir." Duke Ellington explained. "I guess word travels fast when there is a coronation taking place."

"Dale, who do you think, is going to win?" The king asked.

"It does seem that they are both outmatched for each other," Dale replied.

"How can you say that," asked Ellington. He was certain he knew that the dwarf was going to be a goner.

"Well, if you look closer, you will see that the dwarf

sits lower on his stead giving him greater balance while the big guy is all force. I think the balance will win over force." Came Dale's reply.

The king studied Dale. "Interesting." He turned to a steward sitting directly behind him. "Put two gold for me on the dwarf."

The steward laughed along with his fellow colleges. "Two gold on the dwarf for the king. I'll gladly take your money, your majesty. He thinks the dwarf is going to win. He must be joking." They laughed some more.

Suddenly the flag was lowered sending the two contestants barreling down their appropriate lanes with lances protruding before them. The big guy missed his mark, while the dwarf hit the opponent just before the week spot in his chain mail. Apparently he had noticed the flaw in the armor too.

They repositioned their steeds and waited for the flag to be dropped once again before taking off at a canter. This time the larger of the opponents hit his mark in the shoulder, but as Dale explained, he did not lose his balance and remained on his stead's back.

The dwarf missed his mark and was the only result from the opponents contact.

Once again, they took their places and waited for their signal. This time the dwarf not only hit his mark, but he hit it in the desired place. Not only did he unseat his opponent, but he also managed to impale him.

The big guy was not dead yet. This was a match to the death, if the King requested.

"Is this to be a death match, your majesty?" the dwarf asked.

It was clearly who the winner was in this match. But the duke knew what could make men change their own stakes. He nodded to the guard who watched over Treea, which signaled that he bring the woman into view. Were the men after riches or beauty?

The burly man pulled the lance from his abdomen and sought out another weapon. The duke pointed out to him. "There is your answer."

A cheer rose from the crowd. Chants came from both sides of the field. Chants for those who wanted to see one opponent win over the other that in turn changed to, "to the death."

The dwarf had all he could do to duck and roll out of the opponents charge. He had no weapon, except for that of his hands, feet, and quickness. Rolling to and fro to keep the opponent from sinking his mace into his body.

Then at the appropriate time, with the swing of his legs he brought the burly man down. The jolt of his weight in his chain mail suit knocked not only the wind out of his lungs, but the mace from his hands.

This weapon was quickly recovered by the dwarf and brought down swiftly upon the man's head, smashing his skull.

"We have our first victor!" Said the announcer while he grabbed onto the little man's arm raising it. "Who will be our next contestant to go against," there was a pause while the announcer asked the dwarf his name. "Ben Stout, representing the kingdom of Magmark."

Whooping and hollering rose around the stands while the winners who had placed bets on the contestants were paid. The odds were raised for the dwarf after he had proved himself.

Ben Stout remained in the contest for the next five contestants until he was defeated by the lieutenant, who gave the dwarf a swift clean death. It was nothing less than a beheading for the representative of the Kingdom of Magmark.

"Who will challenge Lieutenant Knox? Do we have any takers or was that our last contestant?"

A murmur broke out from the crowd. Treea

swallowed hard. Was this it? Why didn't Dale come to her rescue? Now that he was named prince was she no longer good enough for him?

The king stood up and addressed the crowd and the announcer. "There is one more contestant. We are just waiting for him to arrive. He should be here soon. Let Lieutenant Knox break for some refreshment while we wait."

"You heard the king. We will wait."

The crowd broke up going off in different directions to get their own food and drink. The match was not over, but many now had money to spend from their own winnings that were burning holes in their pouches. Gobs of sweet breads had been baked for such an occasion, all on sale at the market nearby, that was soon flooded with potential buyers.

CHAPTER 22

"Do you really think he will accept the challenge?" Knox asked the duke.

"Aye." He smirked. "A chance to not only get his freedom back to save his daughter, he'll be here. I'm sure of it."

From the sour look on Dorian Knox's face, he appeared to not be looking forward to his next challenger.

"Why the look, Dorian? Do you not think you will win?"

"I kind of liked the man. I don't look forward to killing him."

Duke Ellington laughed. "How about we pay the sweet miss a visit. It might add some motivation to take away that sour look." He led the lieutenant to where Treea was allowed to sit in the shade of a big elm tree, being fanned by two servants who were assigned to keep her company.

The duke pulled a couple of shillings from his pocket and gave each servant a coin. "Go get yourselves a hunk of bread. We will stay with her." A curtsy from the servants after being handed their shilling had them hurrying away leaving Treea alone with the two men.

Lieutenant Dorian smiled as soon as he set eyes on Treea. He loved women that had cleavage they could show off. She was a shapely lassie and he began to look forward to their romp after the match was over.

Duke Ellington reached for Treea's hand and pulled her to her feet. "This, young lady, will make a fine prize for you. Don't you agree, Dorian?"

"She sure is a beautiful one." Dorian agreed. "She's also the one who cut me that day at the dock. I think I've got a score to settle with her."

"Is the contest over so soon?" Treea asked. She eyed the men, after seeing the duke send away the servants, she feared this was more than a social visit, especially when she recognized the lieutenant who had boarded her ship. He was the one responsible for Hurley's death.

"Nope." The duke said to Dorian, "When you win, do you think you will be able to part with her for an hour or two? Kind of as a repayment for posting your entrance fee."

"As long as she's mine after that or you'll have to enter the challenge yourself." Dorian Knox joked.

"How many more contestants?" asked Treea.

"Do you grow weary of the games or are you in a hurry to be off with me?" Dorian ran a finger over her smooth lips. The feel of them sent a quiver to his loins. He knew what he wanted her to do first with those lips of hers.

"I'm just tired of sitting here waiting. The sun is hot and it's doing damage to my skin." She tried to sound the part of a higher class than she was to mask her fear of what was to come.

"Just so you know, there is one more contestant. We are waiting for him to arrive. Would you like to know who he is?"

Treea wasn't sure if she really wanted to know. Hadn't all the best jousters in the land arrived for the match today. "Is the gold prize that high? Surely they can't be all entering because of me."

"You can be so modest when you want to be," replied Ellington. "The last contestant is someone you know."

It couldn't be Dale. They were waiting for someone to arrive and Dale was already here. She raised a skeptical eyebrow in question.

The duke couldn't stand her not knowing. "Why it is your father, Captain Pellesi. Apparently the king has agreed to give him his freedom if he wins the joust. The lieutenant here has only defeated ten challengers so far. What is one more?" He walked behind her and spoke softly in her ear. "Your father obviously will give his life for you. Isn't that dear?"

The trumpets for the match sounded, announcing the arriving riders. It was time to return to the match.

"I will try to give him a clean, swift death. I promise my lady. I always liked your father. It will be an honor to joust with him today. I will return for you soon. I promise." Lieutenant Dorian said after taking her hand to give it a tender kiss before departing to return to the game.

As soon as the men were no longer in earshot and the servants had returned, Treea whispered a little prayer for her pop. "May the goddess watch over and protect you Pop. I will always love you." A lone tear trickled down her cheek.

CHAPTER 23

Captain Pellesi hadn't been on a horse since he could remember. Funny how sea legs can morph into an anchor to grip the sides of the mount. The fine steed had a broad belly, but his legs had no problem gripping about the girth firmly.

Someone had paid a high price for this horse. That person could have been none other than the king. It was a steed that was suited for a well-armored knight.

There was a time in the Captain's life when he did ride with the King's army. A cut to the upper part of his thigh retired him from duty before the age of thirty years, leaving him to find another form of trade to make his living by.

He had already married Treea's mother while he had been in the King's service. Treea arrived soon after, and he still had not found a means of supporting his family on a regular basis. They were forced to scrounge for food until he found his way to the docks and hooked his first fish.

An old sea captain watched him from the bows of his boat fish from the dock day and night. If the fish were landed, Pellesi would not return for a day or two, depending on the size of the last catch.

Word finally made its way to the ears of the captain that the man who fished off of his dock was in dire need of a job.

"Hey, Matey, I hear you are looking for work. I need a deck hand. Would you be interested?"

Pellesi hobbled over to the old man on his bad leg. It was healing, but slowly, it would never be the same, nor would Pellesi's life be the same after meeting the old sea captain, Salty Skip.

"Aye, I need work. I have a wife and a babe to feed along with this bad leg. I'm not of use to anyone I have come across to this day. What is it that I might be able to do for you?"

"A deck hand is what I need. Someone to help man the sails, hoist the anchor and cook for the crew. My last cook jumped ship in the south for warmer weather." Salty Skip laughed.

"How soon will I be paid? I can't just up and leave my family with no means for survival."

Salty Skip grasped on to his money pouch hanging from his belt and poured a bunch of coins into his hand. Gold galleons and silver coins were held before Pellesi to take. "You will get the rest of your share when we return to dock. This should hold your family for the rest of the year."

Pellesi thought his eyes would pop out of his head while he looked down at what he held in his hand. It was more than enough to take care of his family for two or more years on what they had been surviving on at this very moment. And, there was more where that came from too?

"When do we leave?"

"Be at the dock by sunrise tomorrow. I can't promise you when we will return. We will sail south to the islands. There is a lot of spices and such we sail there to trade for."

A wide grin covered Pellesi's face. His struggles were over. "I will be here at sunrise," he yelled over his shoulder, hobbling away to tell the grand news to his young wife.

"What do you mean you are going to set sail in the morning? Who is going to take care of us? Are you going to abandon us over a mere coin?" Mrs. Pellesi stood with a hand on one hip and the babe cradled against her other hip.

Pellesi thought she would be as excited as he was that their struggles were finally over. He figured all he needed to do was show her the gold galleon and she would be happy knowing that that one coin would give her enough funds to take care of her and the baby for a year. Why was it so hard to make a woman happy?

"But dear, there is so much more." He held the rest of the coins out in his hand to show her what he had. She eyed them and looked about their small cabin consisting of a sitting - eating area - a fireplace to cook over and to keep warm. Along with a straw bed in the corner and a wooden crate to lay the babe down to sleep.

"There's more," he repeated.

She held out her hand to accept the coins. "You say there is more?"

"Aye, the rest will be paid upon my return."

"How long will you be gone?"

"He did not say. All he said was that we were to set sail to the south islands to do some trading and then return. It can't be that long. How far away do you think the islands are?"

She laughed, "I hear they are on the other side of

the world. You will be gone for most of the year at the least." She handed the coins back to him only because the baby had begun to cry. It was feeding time. "The coins will buy food and clothing for Treea and me. But you must promise us that you will return."

Pellesi just about did a jig. The woman was warming up to the idea of his trip, which he had never thought possible a few minutes before by the look on her face.

"Aye, woman, I will not only return, but I will bring us great fortune. I will build you a grand home that will model the greatest castle." He kissed her forehead holding her close to him while she struggled with the babe to find a teat.

"Captain, I can see from here, that they await us." The voice of the guard broke through Pellesi's thoughts of his past. A past of nearly twenty years, where had the time gone? The babe was now a grown woman and his own woman was a ghost of his past. He missed his wife dearly and feared she was scowling down on him for letting things come to what they were. Her words in his mind, "Think before you act," haunted him since the day the guards had arrested him.

CHAPTER 24

The sight of him dueled in the pit of her stomach. A part of her wanted to rush to him and another part of her wanted to scream at him to run. Run as far away from here as he possible could go before they caught up to him or did much worse than imprisoning him once again.

Why didn't Dale do something about this? He couldn't let her pop continued to take part in the jousting match. He weren't in that kind of shape to begin with and now that it had been a few months since he had been imprisoned. Surely he lacked the strength to compete.

But Dale continued to sit by the King's side and act out his part. Or, was she seeing a different side of Dale now that he had found his inheritance?

She hadn't really known him, but she believed in her heart that she was a good judge of character. Maybe she was wrong the whole time and should have gone on with her original plan of kidnapping him as Hurley had wanted. It wasn't like he was a pirate anyway, he would not be following the same code of honor as she or her pop.

The lieutenant was already on his horse and waited at the other end of the field for the competition to begin. Her pop was busy being dressed in some sort of leather armor that didn't appear to be able to deflect the faintest point. He was doomed right from the start.

Treea couldn't watch her pop die right before her eyes. He should have declined and remained in the tower. It would have been better for the both of them. At least if he had been still in the tower, she could have managed to find a way to break him out. Now he was facing almost certain death.

He was given a lance and a helm slid on top of his head. Another rider on a horse similar to his own galloped across the field to stop before her pop. The rider was also garbed in the same attire, right down to the helm and lance. What was going on?

The two, her pop and the newcomer, circled each other stirring up a bit of commotion from across the jousting arena. Cries followed from the crowd to begin the competition and finish the match.

Duke Ellington addressed the king briefly, apparently asking whom the other rider was. More commotion broke out. Soon a flood of horses came rushing across the field from where the last rider appeared.

Treea recognized a couple of the riders as members of her own crew. How they had survived the attack on their ship was beyond her. But somehow they had managed.

A lone figure sat upon a horse off in the distance watching the riders below. Could that be Salty Skip? Treea may never know.

Fighting broke out. The crowd dispersed in a flood of people hurrying back into the city to escape the fighting. With the exception of a few men or women who began helping the new arrivals as they harried at the Duke and King's guards.

One of the riders bore down on her, the one with the leather armor and readied to grasp on to her and pull her up on his horse, but the Lieutenant was there first. He snatched her up by the back of her dress, causing it to ride up. The collar of the dress threatened to choke off her airway. All she could do was allow her assailant to toss her over his horse before him.

She wanted to fight back, but she continued to have trouble breathing. If only she were able to fall from the horse and out of his grasp, she would then be able to recover her wits about her.

Kick, she told herself, kick at the horse. She moved her feet in rhythm against what she thought might be a horse's stomach. Her action worked, not the way she had expected. It reared up and thrashed about the air before it with its front legs. She kicked some more.

The rider struggled to control his mount. One more good kick and both she and the rider were on the ground, the horse ran off into the distance.

With the sudden release of her dress, she was able to regain herself. Just because she was in a dress didn't stop her from battling with her attacker.

He raised his hand to hit her, she countered with a swiping kick, knocking him off balance. His sword lay on the ground three feet away from where they fought.

Treea burst after the sword. She almost made it, only to find her feet pulled out from under her. Her attacker had leaped at her grabbing at her legs in order to prevent her from reaching the sword.

He grappled with her on the ground, attempting to use his body to keep her from acquiring his weapon.

Treea used her legs, bringing them up over his back and around his neck, pulling him off of her. She twisted around, reaching for the sword. As her fingers found the hilt, a boot pressed down on her hand, stopping her from raising her hand.

She looked up. Duke Ellington stood over her.

CHAPTER 25

"Take her. We'll keep her locked away for now. Put her in my bas-tile. I don't want to spare any men guarding her. We will need everyone to round up the captain and his men."

"Aye sir, after the little wench gets a licking from me. I don't take too kindly to being thrown from my horse."

"You will do no such thing. The last thing I want is for her to escape just because you had your pride hurt. I've seen how you give her a licking, looks to me as the one who will get a licking will be you from her," the duke replied. He finished up lashing her hands together with a piece of leather cord off of the horse's saddle. "Do I need to bind her feet too, or do you think you can manage to get her to my tower without a struggle?"

Lieutenant Dorian winced from the chastise remark. "Aye sir, I will do as you wish. She can walk there. I won't chance putting her back on my horse either." He tied his end of the cord to his saddle before urging his horse forward. A slow trot should wear her out.

Treea knew better than to fight the horse's gait. She complied and jogged behind the horse all the way to the Duke's estate made up of carved gray stones. A small fortress that was a fraction of the size of the king's castle, but it was a fortress none the less. It had a parapet around it with wall walks and a double wooden gate that opened outward instead of inward. It was the duke's own design meant to keep attackers out.

Archers lined the meurtrieres ready for any oncoming attacks.

The inners of the estate consisted of four main buildings. A forebuilding led to the keep where the Duke's chambers were and a tower off to the west wing was where the bas-tile was located. This was where the lieutenant took Treea.

As was expected, Treea was exhausted from the jog all the way to the castle. She was no trouble for the lieutenant. He didn't lash her as he wanted to, but settled for a little bit of rough treatment when he shoved her into her cell. With a knife he carried in his belt pouch, he slashed the cord from her wrists while he held tightly to them. Just before he shoved her in the cell, he made a thorough effort to twist her wrist making her cry out in pain before releasing her and locking the door.

This was where she would stay. He knew he would be able to come back at a later time, maybe in the night, and regain some of his pride that she had taken from him that day.

Right now, the duke had other plans for him. She was to be here for safe keeping. A little bit of leverage between the duke and the pirate captain.

Now, it was time to round up his men.

CHAPTER 26

Riders on the horizon alarmed the king's guard. They appeared to come out of nowhere. "Get the King and Prince out of here at once." Guardsmen barked to his men.

Dale wanted to stay. He would have fought beside the king's men, it wasn't as though he didn't know how to fight. But he and the king were not dressed or prepared to fight. Instead, they were ushered off and returned to the castle.

As he was taken away, he spied the rider barreling down on Treea, but at the same time, another rider was hurling toward her. Then he realized the other rider was the Duke's lieutenant as he grabbed a hold of Treea's dress and hauled her up in the rudest fashion on the back of his horse.

That was not a rescue on the Lieutenants part that was a capture as far as Dale was concerned. Why was the Duke holding Treea? What did he think he was going to gain by doing so?

Surely the Duke didn't think that Dale had taken a liking to the pirate's daughter and think he could use her against him. But Dale did find himself to continue looking back over his shoulder as he was whisked away with the king. He tried to watch to see which direction the rider bore her off in, but he really couldn't tell. His suspicion was the Duke's estate. That would be the most logical place for the Duke to keep her.

"That was a bad move on my part." The king said while he led Dale to the solar room off the south side of the Hall. "I should have known that by releasing Pellesi just for a single moment from the prison, his men would show up to rescue him."

Dale couldn't help but ask, "Why was he arrested?"

"I was told he brought me bad cargo." The king explained. "You can't take payment for bad cargo and not agree to repay your merchant when the goods are considered bad."

"What kind of cargo was it?"

"I'm not sure. I was told that he brought us nothing but rat poop. I had the cargo burned."

"You burned the cargo?" Dale had an inkling of what the cargo had really been. "Who told you that the cargo was bad?"

"Ellington. He and his men were present when Pellesi presented the sacks to the merchant. The payment was made. Pellesi had left before the sacks were opened to reveal that the contents were nothing but rat poop."

Dale couldn't help but laugh. "You burned a precious cargo?"

"Rat Poop, how can rat poop be a precious cargo, unless you are planning on starting the next epidemic?"

"I have a feeling, from what you just described, that was not rat poop, but nothing more than cocoa beans."

"I've never heard of cocoa beans."

"Of course not. The cargo was so precious, they

are usually only traded on the black market to the inn merchants. It looks exactly as you describe. When it is dried and ground, it has a taste that isn't comparable, not even to coffee. We both know how coffee is a rare commodity in our kingdom too. Didn't Pellesi bring you sacks of coffee once?"

"If that is the case, then wouldn't Ellington know this too?"

"I would think so. Maybe he has other reasons for wanting Pellesi captured. Could he be up to something and Pellesi knew about it?"

"How can you say something like that against the Duke. Such and accusation would be a reason for treason for either you or him."

"I think you should consider the possibilities, though."

"How could I do such a thing? He is my trusted brother. He's been there for me even after our parents died."

"Treason or not. I do believe there is more to Duke Ellington than you know. I would investigate the possibility that the rat poop wasn't rat poop. If you found out differently than you would have cause to be suspicious."

"You do have a point, and I know just the person to investigate the matter." The king turned striding toward a man guarding the outer doorway to the solar room. "Bring me Girdy. I have a mission for her."

CHAPTER 27

"Your majesty, I have the item you requested." Girdy offered up a small cloth sack for him to take.

"This is what is left of the burned cargo?"

"Aye, it is all I could recover from the ashes." She watched while he opened the bag to inspect its contents.

"It looks like rat poop." He asked Dale, "Is this not rat poop?"

Dale took the sack from him and looked at its contents. Pulled a single bean from the bag. Sniffed it and proceeded to place it on his tongue to the King's horror. "NO, it isn't rat poop. Sure enough, it is cocoa beans. They do look alike, don't they?" He removed another bean and offered it to the king. "Here, try one for yourself."

"Ooo, might I try one?" asked Girdy.

The king continued to watch in horror while Dale and Girdy placed another bean in their mouths demonstrating that the beans were not in fact rat poop as he had been told by Ellington. He reluctantly accepted a bean from Dale and tried it.

Surprise... Just as Dale had said, it wasn't rat poop, though the king didn't know what rat poop tasted like, but sure enough, it couldn't possibly taste as good as this. "Why would Ellington insist that these bags contained rat poop?"

"Your majesty, there is something I've wanted to tell you for some time, but I don't know," Girdy said quickly. She looked about the room making certain the three of them were alone.

"What is it Girdy? Illegal trade?" The king asked.

"No... far worse."

"Now what can be far worse than Black Market Trading?"

"I'm afraid to tell you. You will say I am a treasoner and will lock me up. If I'm to tell you then, you need to promise me you won't be angry with me." Girdy fretted.

"I trust you Girdy. What is it that you know? You have been my eyes and ears for years. Go on, tell me."

"It is about Duke Ellington."

"What about Duke Ellington?"

"He is planning on taking your throne."

That got the King's attention. "What did you say? How can you say such a thing?"

"You promised, you wouldn't be mad at me."

"What proof do you have? Girdy, I'm not mad at you, but what you are saying is hard on my ears."

"It's the truth. I've over heard him making his plans for how he is to take the throne."

"Does make sense. First the burning of the beans to remove Pellesi. He knows that Pellesi would have come to my aid even though he is a pirate."

"There's more...," Girdy added.

"What else do you know?"

Dale began coughing. A little bit overly purposeful, but it did get the Kings attention in time to see Duke

Ellington enter the solar room.

"Girdy, excuse me. Now be a good little servant and bring that tea I just requested to my chamber. I will want it in the library." He turned to Dale. "Son, you need to get checked out with a physician. Make certain that cough of yours isn't something serious."

Dale bowed as Girdy did so. The two of them hurriedly left the room. On the way out, Dale did make a quick note in the guard's ear to be wary of Ellington when he was in the King's presence. The guard raised a suspicious eyebrow at Dale, Girdy and the Duke. The idea of the Duke being dangerous sounded absurd. Who could think of such a thing?

A quick shrug on Dale's part was the only response Dale gave the guard before he hurried away. Leaving the guard keeping a watchful eye over the king and the duke.

CHAPTER 28

"Is there something you wish to say, Ellington?" The King turned his back on the Duke to gaze out the long narrow window of the library. The cocoa bean taste lingered in his mouth reminding him of how Ellington had claimed that the shipment Pellesi had presented was not indeed rat poop but that of a very fine discovery of cocoa beans.

"The pirate, Pellesi, has escaped by the aid of his men and some other mercenaries. I am rounding up my troops. We will have them captured soon."

Ellington continued, "I think a round of whippings would suffice in the common for all to see after that display that ruined the jousting match and the celebrations of the day."

The king walked about the room, hands clasp behind his back, deep in thought. "Ellington, what charges were brought against Captain Pellesi?"

"Why, fraud and deception. You already know this. Why do you ask? You agreed and ordered his arrest."

"No, Ellington, I don't remember what his charges were, what was his fraud? His deception charge?"

"Bad cargo, you know this?"

"What made you so sure that his cargo was bad?"

"I saw it with my own eyes. It was nothing more than bags of rat poop."

"What would you say if I told you that the so called rat poop wasn't rat poop. What would you say if I told you that rat poop was a shipment more valuable than salt from the mines or this here tea I'm drinking?"

Ellington's eyes grew wide. "I'm absolutely sure that the shipment was rat poop. We burned it all for fear of a plague running through our kingdom."

"You never showed me evidence that the shipment was rat poop."

"Since when do I need to prove anything to you?"

"I am your King, have you forgotten?"

"I haven't forgotten. But I am your elder and a council member. I have every right to overrule any of your decisions, even the decision to take that vagrant who claims to be your long lost son, into the family. You can't be serious. A Vagrant can't be king. The people will not follow him. He has no education. Not even any fighting skills."

"Ellington, you know nothing about the boy, nothing at all. I know for a fact that he is my lost heir. Vagrant or not, it doesn't matter. He is my blood and that is all that is needed to pass the crown on to him."

"He is only half royalty blood. I'm full blood. I should be crowned instead, and you know it." Ellington stood within inches of the King's nose.

It would be a mistake on the King's part to back down. "You will never be crowned King - Ellington." He stepped closer invading Ellington's space forcing him to step backwards.

"Then my lands will not support the crown any

longer." Ellington rested his hand on the hilt of his sword, drawing the attention of the guard at the doorway.

"Escort Ellington from the castle. And make sure he takes all of his men with him too."

The guard drew his sword, keeping it ready to strike if Ellington decided to put up a fight.

Treachery in the castle. The king wondered how long it had been going on. How long had that goblin, Girdy, known about Ellington's plans.

Something nagged at him about Captain Pellesi. He needed to get to the buccaneer before the duke found him. He was certain Ellington planned on killing the captain. Did the captain know other secrets about Ellington? Could that be the true reason behind why he had kept him locked up?

The king continued to ponder over the events of the past that Ellington had his hands in while he made his way to the Keep. The captain of the guard was busy oiling his blade.

"Conrad, I want you to take some of your men and see if you can find Captain Pellesi. Hopefully, you can get to him before Duke Ellington. I believe he wants him dead. When you find him, I want you to bring him to the castle for questioning. Don't treat him like a prisoner."

"What if he refuses? What then? Do I bound him in order to bring him in?"

"No." The king thought for a moment. "No, don't bring him in. Meet with him in private. Warn him that the Duke wants his head. Then tell him that I want to meet with him. I believe he has answers to questions I need to be answered. I promise to meet with him in secret. Can you do that?"

"Aye. I know who to take with me." Conrad stood, sheathing his sword. "There has been talk about the castle about Duke Ellington."

"So you say. How long has this talk been going on?"

Conrad avoided eye contact. "I can't say. It would be treason for me to do so, by speaking ill of the Duke."

The king clasp his hand on Conrad's shoulder in the manner he would to a good friend. "Conrad, you wouldn't be speaking treason. Duke Ellington has withdrawn his support from the castle."

Conrad's eye went wide. "He will be rallying his forces soon."

"Conrad, are you still with me?"

"Aye, your majesty." He dropped to one knee. "Forever and always, you are my King, and I will forever stand beside you."

"Good. Find me Pellesi before Ellington takes his head."

CHAPTER 29

Treea fell onto the floor with a force of the hand of Lieutenant Dorian. This time she was in a dirty cell in the basement of the tower. No chains. No bedding. It was damp, cold, and dark. The only light filtered through a small hole in the door, that was coming from a single torch outside her cell.

No sound, except for that of water dripping from the ceiling on the other side of her cell. That would mean that if she could find the drip then there would be some water to drink. If she wanted to keep her strength for as long as she could, she would need to stay hydrated.

She didn't really want to call on the sea goddess. Being underground, they would know without a doubt that she was a witch. Treea wanted to escape, not be burned at the stake.

Because she had all the time in the world, she began to slowly grope about the room. At first she found nothing but mud, then her hands found a skull. It had been there for some time. Animal or human? Animal -

maybe a rat. Rat's could feast on her, or - she could feast on them if no one brought her any food.

Move on - A piece of wood. A small broken board. Why a board would be found in the cell with her, she couldn't fathom. It did have a sharp edge to it. A possible weapon. She stashed it by the wall near the skull.

Now her eyes were beginning to adjust to the darkness. A bucket - in the middle of the room. A sniff told her it had once held excrements, maybe blood.

Could someone have been beheaded in this room? Ghosts? Treea believed in ghosts. She wasn't afraid of them, but just the same, she took the board and scratched a pentagram in the mud in hopes of it keeping her safe from harm. Hopefully, no one would notice.

Footsteps sounded on the stairs. Treea rushed to a corner away from the door. The board hid behind her back.

Keys jingled in the door opening the lock. Moisture had taken its toll on the hinges. "Oh beautiful, I'm here for you." Lieutenant Dorian waved the torch about the room in search of her. "Oh, there you are. Don't be afraid. I've come to take you from here. I know of a place much nicer. Cleaner - with food and no rats."

Treea waited. She waited for him to get closer. When he reached for her arm, she thrust with all her might, that board that she held behind her back, right into his chest, as close to his heart as she could aim for.

Her attack was a surprise that she took full advantage of. She pushed him out of the way, ripping the keys from his hand. The torch had fallen on the floor, this she retrieved. He staggered to follow her, but his wound made it hard for him to continue.

She pulled the door shut behind her, leaving him in the darkness. Following the stairs, she extinguished the torch before she was half-way up the stairs. Taking great care with the door, as silently as she could, she let herself out while the guard was away from his post, chatting with another comrade.

In the courtyard, soldiers spared against each other for practice. Several laughed when an opponent fell to the ground at the efforts of the other. Apparently he wasn't very good.

Treea was at odds. She needed to cross the courtyard without being seen. A woman, the chambermaid, walked past her in a hurry. The only thing Treea could think to do was to follow her as though she were with her to aid her fetching the water from the well. Fortunately, the maid never noticed her.

Bushes clung tight to the wall where the well was located. This was where Treea disappeared behind the foliage, waiting for a chance to escape undetected. The sun would be setting soon. Hopefully, they wouldn't discover the missing man in the dungeon before she made it to safety.

Forget being burned at the stake for being a witch. Instead, she would be either hanged or beheaded for killing a man.

During the past days, Treea kept thinking about Dale. Had he forgotten about her? Did he really intend on entering the jousting match to save her from the Duke?

Had the king actually believed his story about being a long lost heir?

What about the Duke? Why did he want to keep her captive?

Did they kill her Pop for escaping or had he managed to get away?

The answers to these questions would have to wait. All she could do was hope for the best. Right now, she needed to find safety. The ship wouldn't be the place to go. It had been torched in the harbor the night the Duke's men captured her. If her pop saw his ship, he would probably cry. Would he whip her for it?

Young lady, you take what you get. If you get out of this alive, be thankful he would be alive to give you a whipping.

Imagine if he learned about her and Hurley? Talk about being in trouble. She wasn't sure what he would do if he found out.

Before she knew it, darkness crept across the sky. She had to make her move. It was now or never.

Foot traffic continued to leave the castle keep, crossing the courtyard. Treea had to slip from the brush without looking as though she were a fugitive. Blending in took a lot of effort on her part.

She needed to match strides as she broke from the bush, or they would notice where she came from.

The main gate was still open. Hope shook every nerve in her body. A large group of citizens was leaving the grounds. Somehow she managed to slip in with them and look the part of a servant. She didn't smell any better or worse than they did, thank the goddess for that.

A single torch bearer led the way to the edge of the town, the town where Treea met Dale. It was also where her ship had been a blaze in the harbor thanks to the hands of the Duke.

The dark alcove of a side street offered her sanctuary. No one noticed her missing. Somehow she needed to get off the street before daylight. The last thing she wanted was to be seen by someone loyal to the duke. This point, she couldn't trust anyone. There was no telling how much hold he had on any of the townspeople.

Even the innkeeper couldn't be trusted. The stables would only provide safety while the sun was gone. Riders would be in and out of the stable making it impossible to hide.

Where else could she go?

If only her ship were still in one piece. She needed food and water. A bath would be nice since she stunk like a pig. Her hair, still pinned up on the back of her head, was quickly growing into a thick mat from caked mud.

Yellow eyes appeared out of nowhere. The scent of maple and apple filled her nose. Sickly sweet odor wanted to make her empty stomach turn. Treea was found quicker than she had imagined. With a start, she almost reached out to grab the attacker by the throat while a gasp started to escape her lips in automatic response to being surprised.

Thick, calloused fingers covered her mouth causing her hand to reach up to pull away while the attacker hushed her to silence. Whispering, "Quiet you, or you'll get us both killed."

The attacker then grabbed her by the arm and pulled her into the building behind her through a locked door. Treea followed in silence. Did they know who she was? Who's side were they on?

A single thick candle lit a room at the top of the stairs. One bed, one table and one chair adorned the room. The attacker directed her to the chair. Was she about to become gagged and tied?

The plate of food sitting on the table was pushed in her direction while the attacker filled a tin cup with some sort of liquid. Treea was afraid to speak. She didn't want them to know that she wasn't some sort of a homeless beggar she appeared to be.

The candle was moved to the table. It brightened the room showing the goblin standing before her. Girdy. Treea knew Girdy and Girdy knew her. "How?" Treea began to ask.

Girdy once again hushed her and pointed to the food and drink on the table. Food that wouldn't be poisoned nor drinks that would be tainted. The goblin was a good friend of her Pop's.

Why she had even bothered to try and ask was

beyond her. She knew that Goblins had a knack for knowing the unknown. One of the reasons why the creatures were so mysterious.

Treea continued to eat in silence. Watching, waiting for an explanation to come forth from the Goblin's lips.

The goblin produced a long black cape, giving it to Treea. "Wear this. We are riding out of here before they come for you."

Treea didn't argue. She knew better and that cape did more than hide her features. No one would know who was underneath it unless they made her remove the hood. A part of her feared that the goblin would turn her into the Duke. Another part of her continued to trust the goblin she had known for years. Why else would she feed her? A starving prisoner lacked strength to battle off any attacker.

Two horses waited behind the stable in the dark of the night. No moon. No light. Not even a torch. All they had were the stars above to guide them and a rope joining one horse to the other - lead.

After a couple of tries, Girdy helped Treea up onto the horse. The food and drink had not yet repaired her strength. It had been a few days since she had a restful sleep. As soon as she was mounted, the animal lurched forward, being led by the lead.

When Treea realized they were going in the direction of the castle, she wanted to bail off the horse. The duke was probably waiting for them around the next bend. How could she have trusted the goblin so easily? Hadn't her pop taught her anything?

The gate to the castle grew closer. "I can't go there. They'll kill me." Treea tried to unleash the lead on the horse's halter. The clip would not open. They were even closer to the gate.

"Quiet!" Hissed the goblin. "You'll get us both killed." They stopped by the side of the road on the edge of the woods. "I've been ordered by the King to bring you to the castle for safe keeping. Lucky for me that you managed to escape. Unlucky for you that they discovered the corpse and the symbol etched in the mud. The duke was going to behead you. Now, it will be the death by fire."

"Do you want to live, or burn?"

Treea didn't think she had made that pentagram that noticeable. But then again, they probably had searched the cell for clues as to how she had managed to escape. What did the King have planned for her? The goblin did say safe keeping didn't she?

"Let's go before they see us." Girdy whipped the horses around and broke out into a trot, almost unseating Treea from the sudden gait change.

"You there, halt!" Ordered the gatekeeper as they entered inside the castle grounds.

Girdy showed her yellowish teeth with a snarl. "I bring the package to the King as ordered."

"Girdy, I didn't know it was you until now. Proceed. Leave your horses with me, I will see that they are tended to."

"Conrad, thank you." Girdy dismounted and helped Treea down off the horse. "I would close the gate. They know the package is missing."

"Damaged?"

"The damage was done to Lieutenant Dorian."

"There will be hell to pay for that damage. I'm sure he got what he deserved." Conrad held the leads to the horses, handing them off to a stable hand appearing out of nowhere, hidden by the darkness.

Girdy didn't bother to reply. The goblin continued on into the Keep while Treea followed close behind. Apparently she knew the castle well. They passed through many doors Treea had never known existed.

Finally, they entered the bath house. Handmade

marble pools glistened in the torchlight of many torches hanging on the walls around the vast room. Only one of the pools contained water that steamed in the cool air.

"Bathe yourself. I will be back to take you to a room for your accommodations. Don't speak to anyone or risk the Duke knowing you are in the castle. Clothing on this bench is for you. I will be back soon."

The whole day had Treea off kilter. First the joust match, then her Pop showing up for the contest. Then the Duke holding her kidnapped in his dungeon. She never once suspected the goblin Girdy to have the access she had to the king's castle.

How many years had she and her Pop known the goblin who she thought was just a waitress at the Inn where her Pop had been arrested? She wondered what her Pop knew about Girdy, was the goblin a spy?

Treea continued to wonder about the day's events while she stripped down naked to enter in the warm water of the pool. It felt good on her bruised, cut skin. Even though her cuts stung, she welcomed the pain. She was alive.

CHAPTER 30

"What do you plan to do with her?" Conrad asked while he poured the king and himself a glass of wine. A table covered in fruit, cheese, and drink had been set up by the servants outside the stable, allowing the King to observe Dale's riding lessons. Later would be fencing lessons with Conrad, and the king planned to continue his observations.

"First I'm going to question her. I want to know why she had a change of heart and let him," the king pitched his thumb in the direction of Dale while he spoke quietly, "go?"

Squinting slyly at Dale, Conrad replied, "You do know what he was doing for a living?"

"No, I don't. He hasn't talked much about himself. He mostly talks about his mother, as though he is trying to prove her existence. The more he talks, the more I become skeptical that she still lives. Especially when he talks about her in the past tense."

"I do know him. He's been living a pretty shady

lifestyle."

"You don't say? How so?"

"I think you should breach that subject with him. It is best that it doesn't come from me."

"If you had a choice of who was to rule the kingdom if I were to die, whom would it be?"

"I'm sorry, your majesty, I'm not your counselor. I wouldn't be able to make such a decision."

"But, you're not making a decision. I just want to know, who do think is the most capable of running the kingdom?"

Conrad grinned. "Treea of course."

The king laughed. "She's no relation."

"What a shame."

"What do you know of this woman?"

"She can outfight the best of my men - level-headed - and an inner strength that is unmatched by anyone I know."

"Do you know why the Duke wants her so badly?"

"There is a war between Captain Pellesi and the Duke. What it's all about, I haven't the faintest clue.

Dale returned to the king's side with the riding instructor. "He did well today for his first lesson, even though he says he's never been on a horse. I find it hard to believe. Do you wish for him to have more instruction tomorrow?"

"Tomorrow?"

"Yes, your majesty, the horse is tiring and should be allowed to rest and eat."

"Go then, tomorrow is another day." The king turned toward Dale. "Are you still up for that fighting lesson?"

Dale looked Conrad over. "I think I could manage a sparring session or two."

"Then let's do this." Conrad flung a wooden training sword at Dale and appeared surprised when he caught it in mid-air. He raised his weapon and took his stance and waited for Dale to do the same, but that never happened. Dale stood as he always stood and held the sword straight up and down in front of him as though he were a child examining a new toy.

"Are you ready to fight or are you going to just stand there?" Conrad asked.

Dale remained as he was. "I'm ready to fight. What are you waiting for?"

"I'm waiting for you to put your feet right and to hold your weapon properly."

Dale looked down at Conrad's feet and moved his own by only a slight bit. They still appeared to be as they were before. His hands he shifted slightly down the hilt. Not much of an improvement.

The king wanted to laugh. He wasn't sure if Dale were toying with Conrad or if he actually didn't know how to fight. Conrad grimaced in frustration. He started to lecture Dale about his stance. "Just take the first swing, Conrad. Show him why he shouldn't stand that way."

Conrad obliged gratefully. He swung with all his might, Dale merely stepped aside causing Conrad to fall off balance and miss his mark. The king couldn't stop laughing. "Will the two of you stop playing and start sparring."

Conrad decided to take a different approach. He swung his weapon before him with careful aim making contact with Dale's. While doing so, he spoke. "The king wants to know what you have been doing for a living?"

"I'm a caretaker." Dale swung his weapon with ease and matched Conrad swing for swing.

"That's a different way to put it. I know for a fact that you're not a caretaker of the same sense. You do not handle dead bodies and put them in graves."

"I can if I need too."

"What do you really take care of?"

"I take care of my mother. She is a wonderful woman who has very little and makes do with what she has."

"I know for a fact that you're a mamma's boy. Now tell the king what you really take care of?"

"I don't know what you mean? I'm not a mamma's boy. I can't help it if I never had a father."

Why wouldn't this boy play fair? He broke the rules of stance and held his sword all wrong but continued to counter strike for strike without tiring or losing his balance.

"Tell him how you're a Gigolo. That's right, tell him what you really take care of."

"So what, I take care of other people. I meet their needs. When was the last time you did something for somebody, not because you had to, but because you wanted to.

The king laughed once again. "Conrad, you mean to tell me that you're worried because he's a Gigolo?" He stopped laughing to ask, "Men or woman?"

The question surprised Conrad more than it surprised Dale.

A sly smile formed on Dale's lips. "Women of course."

The king laughed once again. "He's well educated for his wedding night."

Conrad lunged one last time at Dale. He wanted to throw him off his mark and send him down on the ground. Reverting to using his own leg to sweep Dale off his feet, he was finally able to pin him to the ground with the tip of his weapon. "Bah, you're nothing but a man whore!"

Not waiting for the king to dismiss him, Conrad stomped away.

CHAPTER 31

"I don't think anyone suspects anything." The king said softly. Duke Ellington gazed out the open window at the forest below. "And, you're sure no one followed you back to the castle?"

"That, I'm sure of," replied the Duke. "Lieutenant Dorian is dead. He won't pose a problem for us. Are you sure Conrad doesn't suspect anything?"

"He doesn't appear to suspect anything. He is more worried about whether I will be crowning my Heir to the throne. No one knows. Except for Captain Pellesi."

"We will deal with him once and for all. My men are bringing him in now. I'll personally make sure he doesn't speak a word."

The king turned to face Ellington. "We can't have him ruining all our plans."

"I still can't believe you sold the kingdom to the Norbese Clan. All for what? It couldn't be money? The kingdom has plenty of money."

"At the time, I didn't have an heir. They promised me

retirement in paradise. They will arrive in a day or two to take me to that tropical island to live out the last of my days surrounded by women. What more could I ask?"

"You're no longer interested in Dale's mother?"

"She's probably old and flabby by now. I've moved on. Granted, I did love her at that time in my life, but that was many years ago. Why do I want to take care of an old woman when I can take care of young beautiful women?"

"The sun is about to rise, I better return to my estate and prepare to go to battle with you. Hopefully, you'll be right about the Norbese coming soon. I wouldn't want you to be accidentally killed in our little mock war."

Girdy had slipped from the shadows of the room before she was detected. A fly on the wall buzzed away at her approach in the dark hallway inside the castle wall. Only the goblins who built the castle hundreds of years ago knew the passageways existed. Using them to spy, in hopes of one day regaining their beloved castle.

Some humans treated Girdy like a filthy animal while others like the likes of Captain Pellesi welcomed the likes of her. He treated her as though she were a human and not a monster as some did.

It was Girdy who found Salty Skip to come to the Captain's aid at the jousting match. She knew what Treea meant to him, he would do anything for his daughter. Anything at all.

She had delivered the woman right into the King's hands. Had she known they were up to something as odd as selling the kingdom, she would have taken her elsewhere?

There was only one thing she could do, she would have to go to Dale and tell him what she had learned tonight. They had to get him and Treea out of the castle safely. Captain Pellesi would know what to do about the

King and his brother, the Duke.

You just can't sell a kingdom like that. It wasn't right. Wars happen, but selling a kingdom, they must be mad.

"Dale, you need to leave the castle at once. I don't think it will be safe here for you nor Treea."

"What are you talking about? I'm about to be crowned in the next few days."

"You're not going to be crowned. It is all a ruse. The king sold the kingdom to the Norbese Clan and the Duke is in on it too."

"What? Are they mad?"

"I would ask the same question."

"How do you know that the duke is in on the plan?"

"I overheard him making plans with the King. They've been putting on some sort of ruse to bluff the people." Girdy continued, "The Captain knew about the sale, apparently, that is why they imprisoned him. Now they want to make it so that he can't talk. They probably plan to kill him."

"We have to get Treea and go warn him."

"Hopefully, we aren't too late. The duke claimed that his men were bringing him in."

"I still find it hard to believe that the Duke is in on it. He wanted the kingdom for his own. It's not just the way he said it, there was a look in his eye."

"The duke doesn't care anymore about the kingdom than the king does. He may want power, but he's never been happy. He's probably looking to find happiness in another land." Girdy led the way to where Treea was bathing in the bath house. "Either way, we need to get out of here before it is too late."

CHAPTER 32

Treea finished tying the sash around the waist of her dress just as Girdy and Dale entered the bath house. Their sudden appearance surprised her.

It had been weeks since she'd last laid eyes on Dale. Living in the castle hadn't appeared to change him one bit. At least on the outside. The rest had yet to be seen.

Treea curtsied. "What brings the new prince for a visit?"

"We have to go." He looked behind to make sure no one was coming after them.

"What? Why? Aren't you about to become King?"

"He's no closer to being king than he was the day you read that diary," Girdy answered.

"What are you talking about? What nonsense! You're about to become King. Girdy doesn't know what she's talking about." Treea retorted.

"Girdy, the king will know we're on to him, is there any way we can get out of here quickly."

Voices sounded in the stairway coming up to the bath

house. Girdy looked about the room and found what she was looking for, a small crack in the wall behind one of the far empty pools. She pushed on a block in the wall causing an opening to appear. She led them through the doorway and closed it from the other side just in the nick of time.

Treea looked about the interior hallway. It was dark, hard to see. No torches, no windows, just a few cracks in the wall offering up a tiny bit of light here and there.

Since Girdy knew the way, all they needed to do was stick close to her.

A commotion broke out while they remained in the walls. From the sound of the confusion, part of the commotion was about the missing pirate's daughter. The Duke was demanding her to be brought to him at once.

Why would he still want her if he were in on the sale of the Kingdom with the King?

They continued to travel through the walls of the castle. As they were about to exit the wall in the stable, the king's voice traveled to their ears. "Forget the girl and boy. Get me to that ship before Ellington screws things up for us. If the castle is going to get stormed, he may as well be the one they find behind its doors and not I."

They waited and watched while horses were saddled up for the King and his men. The only one not present was Conrad. Where he was, they had no idea. So they continued to wait until the King rode away before making their escape.

One horse was left in a stable, the rest were out in the pasture. There was no way they would be able to fit the three of them on the back of one horse and make it out the gate undetected.

Dale had an idea.

"You there, what have you in your cart?" The gatekeeper asked Girdy.

"Empty grain sacks needing to be filled."

The guard walked behind the wagon and lifted the cloth covering. Sure enough, empty grain sacks filled the back of the cart.

"You're free to go."

Girdy clicked her tongue. The horse's ears twitched back before moving forward at a steady walk toward town. As soon as the castle was out of sight, she had the horse break out into a fast trot. They needed to get to town before the King and his men made it to the harbor. What they would do when they got there, Girdy didn't know. But they had to do something fast.

While they remained under the cover of the sacks hidden from sight, Treea asked if Dale knew anything about the Norbese Clan.

Softly, he told her about them. "The Norbese Clan, rules the continent in the southern hemisphere. Land of the cocoa bean, gold mines, wild beasts, and a pile of gems mounded deep in the bowels of their triangle fortress. Horses and women worked the land while the men waged wars on the continents waiting to be conquered."

"The only ones who stood a chance against the Norbese Army, were the mercenaries - pirates - the likes of Captain Pellesi."

Dale paused while he tried to remember. "In fact, I'm sure, it was the Captain who the King would have had arranged the sale of the kingdom for him without anyone knowing of his doing."

"I don't remember my Pop ever mentioning such a thing. I went with him to this land. All I remember is trading for the cocoa beans. Why would he do such a thing? I also don't remember much about the people. Pop made me remain on board the ship the whole time."

"Compensation, for one thing. I'm sure the king, must have offered him enough so he would be able to sell his ship and finally settle down with you in some undisclosed location, out of reach of the Norbese army."

"That would mean that there had to be one last condition the king required of my Pop before payment would take place. He had to be his bodyguard, and protect him from the Norbese army, or anyone else who might challenge his decision to sell the kingdom."

After what Dale had told the King about Ellington, he was sure the King would be wary about the Duke's final decision. But apparently money talks and speaks the Duke's language. This was an unexpected development. Maybe the Duke wasn't making a move to acquire the throne after all. Could it all have been a ruse to keep them from being found out until after all was, done and over with?

Ellington had been trying for the throne for years. Why the sudden change of heart? Had he grown tired of the games the two of them played?

The Norbese ship was nearing the port. The King could see it from the top of the knoll. He would need to make it to the harbor before his guard noted the ships colors and became hostile to his future buyers.

Where was that pirate ship? Shouldn't it be moored at the pier? He had made certain the captain was released in time to follow through with his end of the bargain. He even made sure that Salty Skip was there to make sure the escape was a success.

CHAPTER 33

Captain Pellesi - the man with too many missions. Dale knew there had been something troubling the man just before he had been grabbed by the king's men and tossed behind a locked door. There was no telling what his role was in all this matter. He just needed to get Treea back to the man before any of this went down. For some reason, Dale believed that Treea was now a pawn in some sort of war game about to take place.

She looked haggard, yet she still pulled at his heartstrings. Why, out of all the women he had been with in the past would she be able to do such a thing? For the past weeks, she had been all that he could think about. He worried about her. She should have been in the home, sitting beside the fire, preparing a meal, with warmth and safety.

Dale could not only take care of his mother, but he could've taken care of Treea too. What was he thinking? He was too young to think about having a family. There was the world to see, a career to gain, schooling to finish.

Apparently, being the heir to the throne had turned out to be a dead end. The dream of it, playing the part for a few weeks had been fun, but he was thankful he wasn't inheriting the headache.

The cart veered off the road toward town and headed toward a hidden cove. Only those familiar with the route would have known of its existence in the dark of night. Soon they were following a sandy shoreline protected by a tall rock formation. A small dinghy boat rested on the shore.

"You need to hurry and get on board the ship before the Norbese makes their move," Girdy instructed. "The captain said for you to follow the five stars, turn left at the third star and you would see the ship not far from there."

Dale looked up and couldn't make heads nor tails of what the goblin was talking about.

Treea immediately raised a small sack from the bottom of the boat and pulled out a spyglass, lifted it to her eye and looked up in the sky seeking out the five stars. "I see them." She climbed in the boat while Dale and Girdy gave it a little push into the water.

Dale managed to hop in before the water became too deep and began manning the oars while Treea continued to point the way to him. He didn't know how she did it, looking like a sea princess by the way she held that spyglass to her eye and her hair billowing out behind her from the sea breeze. In the dead of night, he could make out her silhouette. One word - beautiful.

He must have rowed for over an hour. The sun threatened to rise and expose their existence to the world before the pirate ship loomed in front of them. Voices were heard yelling from the Crow's nest as the crew discovered their approach. A rope ladder was dropped down the side of the ship welcoming them on board. Dale allowed Treea to go first.

Treea was helped over the side of the ship by the captain of the ship and embraced the way a father would hug a long lost child. Captain Pellesi released his hold on his daughter and eyed Dale.

"Pop, he's with me. He helped me escape. We have a long story to tell you, but not now. You have to do something! The Norbese Clan are coming to take the kingdom and I feel something bad is in the air. The duke has something up his sleeve too."

"Aye, child, I know of the Norbese Clan. The king hired me to sell the kingdom for him."

"But Pop, he can't do that, can he? Sell the kingdom? What about the people? The town? What will they do to them? Won't they make them all slaves?"

It was the first time Dale had heard a tremble in Treea's voice. She would be a true princess, she cared about the people. If only he had managed to learn about his heritage before the King had decided to sell the kingdom.

"Calm down, Treea. The Norbese isn't really like that. I don't think their ruler is interested in taking away the kingdom. He was more interested in free trade than anything else. The king wouldn't hear of it when I returned. He told me that I was lying and that I was to stick to my previous agreement, then he tossed me into his hold for safe keeping."

"The Duke is what I'm worried about. He would do anything to keep this free trade from happening. When he learned about the Norbese refusal to purchase the kingdom, he claimed there would be a war on their hands."

"So what are we going to do?"

"There is only one thing to do." Captain turned toward Dale and replied, "Kill the King and the Duke. Treea, you found the heir, so we will still have a King."

Dale said, "You can't be serious. Kill the King? Isn't

that treason?"

"The King has committed his own treason by trying to sell the kingdom and his people. Why should we honor such a man? If his men knew what he had planned, do you think he would still have anyone to back him, protect him?"

"Pop, do we really need to kill the King? What if we only killed the duke and let the chips fall for the King? Wouldn't the Norbese take care of the rest?"

"True, Captain, the man only wants to retire without the responsibility. He wanted to live out his life in some sort of paradise. Though sadly he has no interest in my mother, understandable since time may have erased anything he may have felt when he was younger. That would take care of one problem. Then we would only have to deal with the Duke."

"I think the boy has a point," Salty Skip replied. "This is what I think we need to do." The old captain laid out his plan of action, each of them to play a role. Everyone except for Treea. Captain Pellesi wouldn't hear of his daughter going back into danger. She belonged on board the ship, out of harms way.

Treea didn't want to hear of it. She was a big girl and could take care of herself. She continued to argue with her Pop over the matter until Salty Skip stepped in and told Treea the decision was made. She would be locked in her cabin if she continued to argue. Her jaw dropped but didn't say another word.

CHAPTER 34

Warships gathered around the coast. The kingdom appeared to be prepared for war. Those ships, five of them, were owned by the Duke and were placed at strategic points about the harbor.

Two pirate ships were positioned on each side of the ship from the Norbese Clan as an escort in the harbor. The captain of the Norbese ship had agreed to take the King back to their country as part of the trade agreement and to take very good care of him. They also understood the hostility. The possibility of a Kingdom being sold out from under the noses of its servants was unheard of. What kind of King would do such a thing? Was he that desperate to get out of his position without having to make one more decision?

It was left up to Dale, to be the one with the task of killing the Duke. He didn't want to do it. That is until Treea told him about her capture by him and his lieutenant. How they had come close to violating her. It made his blood boil. No woman had ever made Dale feel this way. He had to revenge her honor.

Two of Salty Skip's men accompanied Dale to the shore with the agreement that they would make sure his mission to take care of Duke Ellington was successful. Their landing point being the cove where the dinghy boat had been left. Not one soul was to be seen on the road leading from the cove or the road toward the town or the King's castle.

Where should they look first for the Duke? His castle, the King's castle or should they look in the town's inn where Captain Pellesi had been arrested.

How could you look for your opponent if you didn't know how to think like them?

While they discussed which way they should go, a group of horsemen approached them at a crossroad. "Seize them!" Conrad shouted at his men when he saw that Dale was one of the three men.

Dale didn't want to fight with Conrad.

Weapons were drawn from both parties. There were more of Conrad's men than there were Dale and his two mates. Without hesitation, the three men stood with their backs to each other in defense.

"What do you want with us? There are more pressing problems than a beef with me over the King's attention."

"That's the problem. The King. What have you done with him? He's not in the castle and neither are you nor the woman. This lead me to believe that you and the woman are up to no good and have taken the King for ransom."

"You're a fool for thinking such a thing." One of Salty Skip's men spat on the ground before him. "Your precious King is about to sell your Kingdom to the Norbese Clan. Is that what you want?"

"What are you saying?"

"That's right! He's selling the Kingdom as we speak." Dale added.

Swords began to lower slightly at the news. "Then what are your plans?" Conrad asked.

"We plan to stop the sale. Of course, but first, we want to stop someone's plans of war."

"War with whom?"

"The Duke..."

"Why would he go to war?"

"What has the duke wanted all his life?" asked Salty Skip's man.

"The Kingdom." Answered Conrad.

"You're wrong." Girdy appeared out of nowhere. No one saw her approach them from the forest edge.

"What do you know of this you wretched Goblin?" asked Conrad.

"I've watched the King and the Duke for more years than you've been alive. The King has tired of his responsibility to the kingdom. The duke wants the kingdom only for profit. He's never cared about the position, only the wealth that comes with it. Sending people off to war to gain wealth would be his only goal."

Conrad turned and conversed quietly with his men. Decisions...

"What do you plan to do?"

Dale replied, "We need to find the duke and stop him. Taking his life may be our only choice. A ruler that the people will follow needs to be found to take the King's place."

"What about you?" Conrad asked, "You're the heir to the throne aren't you?"

"You know the people know me. What makes you think that they would follow me? You know of my past. I don't think I'm the right person for the job."

"But isn't that why you came forward? To inherit the kingdom?"

"I came forward with the hopes to help a friend in need. Her father was being held captive and I hoped that my influence of being the heir would help free him. He wasn't freed in the manner I had planned, but none the less, my job was done. I'm not a ruler. Just a man with a mission and love for a woman."

"You, Conrad, are the man for the job. The people know you and would follow you." Salty Skip's man added.

Conrad looked about him. Suddenly his men and Salty Skip's men, including Dale were on their knee before Conrad pledging their allegiance to him.

"Led the people." Dale pleaded.

A lone rider approached from the castle. "Conrad! Duke Ellington and some of his men are attacking the castle. The other halves of his men have been sent into town to attack the ships and find the King. Why is the King in town alone?"

"It's begun..." Dale stated.

Salty Skip's man said, "Dale, you ride with Conrad and his men to the castle and take care of the Duke. We will go back to the ship and take care of business as planned."

Dale turned to Girdy. "You go to town and see that my mom stays safe. I have a bad feeling about what the Duke is capable of doing."

"Say no more." Girdy hurried off on her way to the town.

CHAPTER 35

A raid on the castle left parts of the structure engulfed in flames. The stone foundation prevented the rest of the building from burning. A poorly planned raid. Or someone's plans had been stopped. It didn't matter which, just that the rest of the castle still remained intact. The doors were barred from the inside to prevent the Duke from entering.

Ellington could be heard over the clash of swords, ordering his men to remain firm in their fight to take the castle. Even if that meant busting through the door. He wanted to gain entry to the castle.

"Find the King!" He ordered another one of his men.

"Sir, we can't gain access to the castle. It's barred from within."

"Then find something to batter the door down. Do what it takes, I want that man. He's no right to give my heritage away."

"But, you're not the heir so what should that matter

to you?" Conrad said. Sword raised to take on Ellington.

"I'm more than the heir than that harlot. Pig Brain, why do you contest me? You can be me right-hand man."

"I wouldn't want to be your right-hand man any more than a commander of your army."

"So you will be a traitor to your kingdom."

A swipe of the sword across a man's throat proved to be the final strike Dale needed to free himself to join the side of Conrad.

"He's not a traitor, Duke Ellington, you are! I have proof of how you not only killed the Queen, but also prevented her from giving him a child."

"You have no such thing. You're a putrid excuse of a man, no one would listen to you anyway."

"I also know for a fact that you tried to have my mom killed when she found out that she was carrying me. Fortunately for her, she was more resourceful than you were."

The duke continued to exchange sword strike for sword strike. Dale countered with his own sword as he protected Conrad from oncoming challenges of the Duke's men. Would the man never tire?

Dale had thought many times again and again about what it would be like for him to be the ruler of the kingdom. Each time he ran the scenario, it wasn't something that he had wanted. He just wanted to be someone but not a ruler. Maybe a medic, an alchemist or a shop owner, but not a ruler. There was too much headache for him to manage a kingdom, the lands, the servants, or its citizens, not to mention the armies and the trading.

Conrad was supposed to be an expertise swordsman, the leader of the King's army. Why was it taking so long for him to kill the Duke? If they failed, what would become of his mom, Treea, or the kingdom's citizens?

"Come on, hurry up and kill the man and get it

over," Dale muttered to Conrad.

"You think you can kill me?" Duke Ellington swung his sword toward Dale, who easily deflected the strike.

"He's a better swordsman than you might," Conrad replied with a strike of his own to the Duke.

One of the Duke's men came out of nowhere and body slammed into Dale, nearly knocking him off his feet. His sure-footedness prevented him from taking the fall.

The Duke continued to fight Conrad off.

What would Dale do if the Duke killed Conrad? He couldn't let the duke take over the kingdom. A swipe of his sword to his opponent left the man with a gash across his stomach. The man dropped his sword to keep his belly from spilling out on the ground.

Dale turned his attention back to the duke. "You want some help, Conrad?"

"Nay, I got this."

"Don't say I didn't offer to help." Dale deflected an attack from another one of the Duke's men.

The next sound that followed didn't sound right to Dale's ears. Metal hitting and breaking metal. Conrad was down on the ground with the Duke ready to give the final killing swing of his sword across Conrad's throat.

Dale deflected the sword just in time to save Conrad from a beheading from the Duke. But his other opponent finished the job for the Duke. Now it was just Dale and Ellington.

The duke swung again. Dale dropped down to the ground and rolled out of the way. He was back on his feet in a moments time. Elven quickness did come in handy. He then brought his sword low and cut upwards, slicing the Duke from his belly up to his throat. Apparently he wasn't expecting such a swing and couldn't deflect it in time.

Ellington grab at his stomach and his throat in shock,

dropping his sword to the ground. Blood spurted from the wound in his throat along with a gurgling sound of someone attempting to speak with no air. Drowning in his own blood.

"That was for Treea. This," Dale raised his sword to cut off the Duke's head, speaking as he swung. "...is for Conrad."

Duke Ellington was dead.

Shouting...

Men ran around Dale while he remained standing over Ellington looking down on the dead body. The head had rolled several feet away, stopping before one of the Duke's men. The man looked horrified by the sight.

"Putdown your arms, the battle is over." Captain Pellesi stood beside Dale and carefully removed the sword from his hand.

Duke Ellington's men were kneeling down on one knee before Dale. This wasn't supposed to happen. He wasn't ruler material. Conrad, where's Conrad. That man was supposed to lead these people as agreed.

His body lay a few feet away, the top part of his body was covered by a cloth, unlike the Duke, whose head still lay on the ground, displayed before his men.

"Son, you're their ruler now." Captain Pellesi pointed to the men scattered around the grounds.

Dale composed himself. His first words to his new servants, followers. "This place is a mess. Get it cleaned up. And, take care of that." He pointed to the Duke's head. "I don't want to see it ever again."

He didn't want to see their expressions. Dale turned away, the castle door, charred at the base, now stood open, allowing access. He had a kingdom to rule.

CHAPTER 36

Do Kingdoms come with instructions? If only the king were still there, he could continue to teach Dale all about what it takes to rule the land. He couldn't even rely on Conrad helping him. Only a few people knew what the king's action plan had been. Eat, spend money and find a woman. Well, that should be easy enough.

Dale knew many women. He also knew how to spend money. Eating wasn't on his greatest past-times. He loved the food, just not to the extent that the King liked food.

"Shall we plan you a Banquet feast this evening?" The assistant to the cook asked Dale. He was seated in the sun room trying to put together what the Kingdom's finances were. His mother sat beside him. She was better at math than he was.

"Banquet? What for?" Dale asked the servant.

"When the moon is full, the King always called for a Banquet in the Great Hall."

"I hope that it wasn't just for him."

"Nay, just him and his counselors."

That meant the Duke and his men, along with Conrad and a few others.

"The trading has done our Kingdom well, my son."

"So our coffers are full?"

"Full and then some."

Dale pondered. The Tavern in town would meet his needs. He leaned over and whispered something into his mother's ear. She giggled at what he said, nodding.

"Delightful!" His mom replied.

"Do me a favor before planning this banquet of yours. Go to the town tavern and ask them if they would mind doing me a favor by coming to the castle. I would like to request a service of them."

The cook bowed out of the room. They couldn't imagine what the young king wanted with the tavern.

It had been over a month since Dale had last seen Treea. He'd seen her father a few times since then and knew his plans were to stay close to the coast of the city. The man was a sailor, a merchant, but he no longer wanted his daughter to remain living on board the ship with him. It was time she made a life of her own.

Captain Pellesi had paid for an apartment for his daughter in the midst of the city. In an area known for the upper class, this was where he wanted her to live. Not the lower side of town where Dale and his Mum used to live.

Since Dale took over the kingdom, he'd made Captain Pellesi his royal naval captain. It was an honor the Pirate had never expected to be bestowed on him.

CHAPTER 37

Treea spun around in the room before her Pop, showing off the dress she had chosen to wear to the banquet at the Tavern. Many people were given invitations to dine with the new king, and she was one of them.

"Treea, you look beautiful." Captain Pellesi said.

"Pop, I still feel odd being dressed like this."

"Don't you worry, dear, you look lovely." Captain Pellesi held a box which he placed on the Kitchen table. He opened it slowly. Treea couldn't help but gasp.

An amethyst crystal wrapped in a silk cord hung from a thin chain of gold. It was beautiful. Breathtaking... The Captain placed this about Treea's neck, complimenting her white lace dress, tight bodice, full skirt, and puffy short sleeves. Her hair, braided in a fancy, high society fashion, was laced with dried flowers.

"There, you look like a princess."

"Oh Pop. Do you have to jest so?"

"I don't know what you are worried about."

"I'm not the only woman he's to choose from for a

bride."

"We will see in time, won't we?"

The captain draped a shawl over his daughter's shoulders. She needed a husband, the man needed someone who would be able to help him with the functions of the castle. Who better to do so than his daughter, of course.

Treea still held a secret. It was the one thing that kept her from arguing with her pop about being made to live on land instead of the ship. Hurley. She never wanted her Pop to learn about the relationship she had with the man. It would have ruined the way her Pop regarded him. After all, it was taboo for any of them to have had the kind of physical contact that Hurley had had with Treea up until his dying day. She hoped her Pop would never learn about the two of them.

Funny how she didn't think much about Hurley. Maybe she hadn't loved him as much as she'd thought she had. Maybe Hurley had felt the same way too. It was just a thing of convenience and nothing more.

Dale, on the other hand, she couldn't stop him from invading her mind. It didn't matter what she was about, whether it was picking up a needle and learning to make one of those beautiful tapestries or knitting a shawl for to wear while the weather turned colder.

She hadn't seen him much since he took over the kingdom, not having any excuses to visit the castle. There were no heirs to kidnap to hold for ransom. That was now a thing of the past. To bad too. She wished she could hire that heir one last time or go sneaking into the grain cellar with him.

Outside the Tavern, the street was lined with people waiting to be allowed entrance. All these people had been invited just like herself. Half the town had to be there.

From where she stood with her Pop, she could see

the stable area behind the Tavern. It too was cleaned up. There were long wooden table arranged there as well. Maybe her and her Pop would be forced to remain outside. Maybe she wouldn't get a chance to see Dale. She never did get a chance to tell him how she felt about him.

Had she missed her chance?

It wasn't like she'd been that nice to him in the beginning. She did hold him captive for ransom. Would he pick another?

The line slowly moved along. Some people were ushered into the back by the stables while others were seated at the long tables inside the tavern. Dale was nowhere to be seen. Would the new king make a grand entrance? Maybe he wouldn't be attending at all.

Captain Pellesi handed over their invitation and followed the waitress to be seated at the front of the room. Salty Skip sat across from the Captain. Girdy was their waitress.

It made Treea laugh to see her Pop flirt with the goblin. But then, she didn't know what to make of it when she plopped herself down in his lap and placed a big kiss on his lips. That took her by surprise.

Minstrels played in a corner of the room while food was brought out to the tables. It was more food than any of the guests had ever seen in their lifetimes, even Treea. Where was the King?

Were they supposed to eat without him?

Decanters of wine were set about each table to refill goblets as needed. The kegs of ale were set aside for later in the evening. Whispers fluttered from one table to the next. Talk about the new King and what kind of woman would be the best suit for him. Many of the women knew him in more ways than one, bringing giggles with the whispers of un-lady like talk.

Some of this talk bothered Treea. Jealousy? How

could she feel such a thing? She barely knew him. But yet all the women talking about him in such ways made her flushed and troubled.

Loud voices, laughter, came to an abrupt silence when Dale entered the hall with his mother at his side. Wearing a robe of the former kings along with the crown he didn't want to wear. He'd only worn it at his mother's request.

"Thank you, all for coming." He said while he walked about the room as though in search of someone. "As you can tell, our coffers are adequately full and should hold us for the future year. Please except this meal in celebration of our prosperous year." Dale stopped beside Treea's table. "Taxes won't be raised nor lowered, but this feast is to honor all of your hard work."

Murmurs whispered about the tables while Dale took a seat next to Treea. Goose bumps crawled up her arm with him sitting so close to her. She could feel the heat of his body and reminded her of their last night together alone in the root cellar of this tavern.

His hand touched hers gently and gave it a little squeeze. She half expected, half wanted, him to lead her away from the table and back down those stairs to the cellar. Instead, he retrieved a pouch from his waist to open before her eyes. Out of it he withdrew a ring. The clear stone cut in such a way that the sides of it caught the light from the torches lighting the room above. It sparkled as though it were made up of many brilliant stars.

Dale took hold of Treea's hand and held it before him. Again the room fell silent. "Treea, with this ring, would you wed me?"

Her face grew hot. Was she flushed? Treea's hand began to tremble. She never expected. Did he not once look at any other woman seated about them?

Treea was aware of all the eyes focused upon her.

She couldn't find her voice. Was this actually happening? After her holding him captive?

"Me? You want to marry me?"

"I do."

"But I held you captive."

Dale smiled boldly. "You still do, even though you let me walk away, I'm still held captive to this day. The only way I could ever be free is to have you at my side for the rest of my life. Treea, marry me and let us be free to love each other." He slid the ring upon her finger and continued to hold her hand before him, not waiting for an answer.

If she said no, would he take the ring back and banish her and her pop from the Kingdom? Even though she had no reason to say no, she still thought about what his reaction would be if she were to reject his proposal.

Reject, no that wouldn't and couldn't happen. She was as much in love with him as he was with her.

"I will marry you Dale."

Had he been holding his breath waiting for her answer?

A cheer rose around the room. Decanters raised, glasses filled and toasts were made to the newly engaged couple, along with a wink from her Pop. A knowing wink. Had he known about the proposal the whole time?

The wedding was grand. Grander than the banquet that was given at the tavern six months prior when Dale proposed to Treea. Winter snow melt had been replaced by the green growth of the grass, leaves on the trees and the flowers in the royal garden in full bloom.

It was held in the castle garden. Girdy accompanied her Pop along with all the mates from her Pop's new ship. A present from the new King.

Unfortunately, the Captain would be leaving on one last voyage. He was in search of more cocoa beans from the Norbese Clan. It was a trip that only he could make.

Salty Skip was accompanying him to establish a new connection with the people. Open trade was going well. With this next voyage, a flood of goods was expected. Not just cocoa beans. There would be silks and exotic fruits too.

Treea wasn't happy with her Pop leaving her behind as he was. Dale promised to keep her busy while her Pop was away. There was a lot to do before his return. Other bordering lands needed to learn about the goods that would be arriving in the coming year.

After the ceremony, Treea had one question she needed to know before her Pop set sail.

"Is there something I should know about Girdy?"

Her Pop smiled. "Aye, there is and I've been reluctant to tell you. Maybe you should have a seat before I tell ye." He waited.

Treea looked at him expecting him to tell her how Girdy was a spy or how he was a spy. What he told her was not really what she wanted to hear.

He took her hand in his and held it gently. "Two months ago, I made her your step-mother. You're going to be a big sister soon. I want you to be there to help her if she needs help. Can you do that for me?"

She wasn't sure if the news repulsed her or made her happy. But if Girdy were the one to make her Pop happy, then happy was what he deserved. If only he had felt right enough to tell her in the first place instead of hiding his feelings. This reminded her of Hurley. How the two of them had hid.

Should she tell him about her and Hurley? Nay, the man had been through enough.

Treea didn't know what to say. Girdy had been the one to come to her rescue, hadn't she? How long had they known each other? Many years…

"I can do that for you Pop. Just promise me you will hurry back home."

"Aye, I will my child. I'll be home before you know it."

Girdy appeared beside the Captain. "May the Goddess watch over him as she watches over all of us."

ABOUT THE AUTHOR

The Dubious Heir is Lydia's big debut. What began as an impromptu NaNoWriMo Project for 2013 slowly blossomed into her debut novella. She's currently working on her next untitled work. We can't wait to see what imaginative yarn she weaves next!

Lydia is a member of Romance Writers of America (RWA) since 2012. A mother of two grown children, she lives in Southern New Hampshire. The best part: writing more fantasy novels featuring dashing and daring men and women.

Visit Lydia online at her website
https://lydia-clark.com/
where you will learn about up and coming new releases and events in your area.

COMMING SOON!

Another Dashing
and Daring Novel
LADY
from
HAYATA
LYDIA CLARK